CARA COOPER

MISSING IN PARADISE

Complete and Unabridged

LINFORD
Leicester

First published in Great Britain in 2018

First Linford Edition
published 2019

*A catalogue record for this book is available
from the British Library.*

ISBN 978–1–4448–4095–7

Published by
F. A. Thorpe (Publishing)
Anstey, Leicestershire

Set by Words & Graphics Ltd.
Anstey, Leicestershire
Printed and bound in Great Britain by
T. J. International Ltd., Padstow, Cornwall

This book is printed on acid-free paper

Brave New World

'It's one of the safest cities in the world. You'll love it, and I can't wait to get back there.'

Warren had squeezed Bryony's hand the way he always did when she was worried. Then he'd pressed the button on the computer and it was booked. Just like that.

Now she was here. And he wasn't.

As Bryony sat in the back of the taxi, she closed her eyes to block out the chaos of Havana's whizzing traffic. She tried to remember what that protective squeeze had felt like, tried to conjure up the comfort, the security it gave her. Tried to envisage her husband once again, to see the contours of his face, remember what it was like to run her fingers over the roughness of his unshaven chin.

But Warren was a fading memory

and, try as she might, she couldn't bring back his warmth, his strength.

A smaller, softer hand crept over hers.

'Are you all right, Mum? You're not feeling sick, are you? These roads are so bumpy.'

Bryony Kemp opened her eyes and harsh sunlight made her blink. She was living too much in her head these days and she knew it wasn't good for her.

The sun's brightness and the searing heat was crazy in this month of January when she thought of how dark and freezing it had been back home in England just a flight away.

'Fine, absolutely fine. It's exciting, isn't it?'

She beamed a reassuring smile at her daughter. Even after 20 hours travelling her ability to act positively wasn't dimmed.

She was the one who had to be strong now. Now it was just the two of them, herself and Anna. Now all they had was each other.

Bryony looked down at her daughter's fingers covering hers. The nails gaily painted a holiday orange, her hands were nevertheless too thin, too delicate. She looked away. Maybe this trip would encourage Anna to eat more.

Then, as the taxi swung crazily round the corner, the Bay of Havana with its sweeping azure ocean made them both gasp as it opened out before them in a spectacular view.

The coast road with its six lanes of hurtling traffic ran as far as the eye could see, in an amazing curve. The city's modern apartments nestled in an arc looking over the water as if a child-giant playing with yellow Lego blocks on the shore had left them, neat and upstanding.

A wide concrete wall, low enough to sit on, was the only thing separating the cars from the battering, sparkling ocean.

'The Malecón, the wall, it is famous, all tourists want to see the Malecón,' their driver announced in a thick Spanish accent.

Speeding along, taking his hand off the wheel to gesture, he was less bothered with safety than the need to point out the highlights of his home town.

'Look at the waves, Mum, splashing over the wall right across the tarmac. Isn't it fun?'

At that very moment, one crashed in front of the wheels of the taxi, sending spray in at the open windows. It cooled and invigorated them. Anna whooped with excitement as the driver swerved to avoid the whoosh of water.

He laughed and shrugged.

'*De nada,*' he declared. 'It is nothing.'

That was the Cuban way, they just got on with it — hurricanes, being poor, shortages. The people endured all life had to throw at them because they lived in one of the most beautiful Caribbean countries.

The people were fabulously proud of their island which looked longingly and at the same time warily across the ocean towards their old adversary, the United States.

The driver had a huge grin on his face, brown as a polished coconut shell, so it showed the gaps where teeth should have been.

Bryony was delighted to see her daughter happy.

'Do you remember Dad telling us about the Malecón, Anna? He said it's where the Cubans walk on summer evenings, where they enjoy the Caribbean breeze coming off the sea. Where they go to meet each other, sip rum and fall in love . . . '

Bryony felt a stab somewhere in her chest. It was duller now than when she had first lost Warren, less acute but still achingly painful.

Yes. She could cope without him. She would make herself.

Coming on this holiday, fulfilling her husband's wish of seeing the world would prove that she could leave the crippling grief behind her.

The last two years had been incredibly tough. Now she was ready to look forwards not backwards. Thirty-eight was too young to carry the label of widow with her for ever. The only thing was, when you had found your one and only, how on earth could you replace him?

Could you ever replace someone who had literally meant everything to you? Someone you'd vowed to grow old with?

She'd not got around to cancelling the holiday. Warren had been such an organised man. Before his fatal heart attack, he'd booked way in advance. In all the chaos following his passing, Bryony had almost forgotten about it.

Simply surviving without him, taking over all the things which had been his role, handling the finances, learning how to fix stuff around the house, dealing with the funeral, had sucked her of every ounce of strength.

When she had finally surfaced from the mist of his untimely death, helping

Anna focus on her A-levels had become the next priority. Finally, going back to work had been another hurdle for Bryony to conquer. She often felt that dealing with his loss was like running a race she'd been forced to enter, jumping over hurdles she didn't want to tackle.

Two years had now passed since she had received the phone call out of the blue which had shattered her life.

Going away was just another hurdle, the challenge of holidaying alone, just two women in a very alien country. This surely was the final hurdle in the race on the way to her recovery from earth-shattering grief.

When Bryony first reminded Anna about the booking to Cuba, her daughter had been less than enthusiastic.

'Please, can't we cancel? I really don't want to go on our own, Mum, it won't be the same without Dad.'

'But I've left it too late to cancel, Anna. It would be a sin to lose all that money that Dad worked so hard to earn. Besides, Dad would have wanted us to go. He was looking forward to it so much. Let's be brave about it, let's be positive. For him.'

It would give her and Anna a chance to smooth things over. Being a lone parent had made her over-protective.

Anna was now eighteen, an adult, albeit a very young one, happy to hang on to her mother's apron strings, and Bryony was finding it difficult to let go.

The taxi swung into the entrance to the Iberostar Parque Central Hotel.

Bryony had tipped the driver generously. The heat coming off the pavements didn't suit the cold-weather clothes they had worn from England and they were pleased to get into the air-conditioned lobby.

This part of the hotel was true old colonial style. A double staircase in marble led to a gallery from which guests wandered hither and thither, looking down on the lobby which echoed the Cuban jungle with its full grown potted palms. Their branches were studded with curious air plants whose roots dangled down like streamers.

Waitresses flitted here and there, their trays filled with Blue Hawaiians and pina coladas, and drinks in shades of red, orange and lemon, like liquid sunsets.

Bryony was pleased there was a group of Canadians registering before her. It gave her a chance to get herself together. That old familiar feeling of anxiety, which had appeared on Warren's death, had begun to rise in her chest.

There were so many things to lose or have stolen, so many things which could go wrong. Would they have her reservation down correctly, had she brought enough money, would their rooms be restful or noisy?

As the anxiety took hold, she could feel her heart beating faster. Cash, passport, insurance documents, mobile phone, she must have checked them all a hundred times since they had left home.

With the lightness of youth, Anna seemed supremely oblivious to such things. Her blonde hair and bright hazel eyes had caught the attention of a young man and Bryony could hear them conversing in German, the language Anna had studied for her A-levels.

It was great Anna had found someone to talk to but Bryony wished she could be more practical. Instead, breezily, she left everything up to her mother.

Oh, how Bryony missed Warren and the way he'd take control of every situation. Now she was the one in control, or she should have been.

Only she couldn't find her passport. Sweat began to bead on her brow. Why wasn't Anna helping? How could she stand there chatting, oblivious to her mother's difficulties?

Suspicious Stranger

Mark Greenstreet twisted the receipt the waitress had given him into a bow shape, then unwrapped it again. He was bored. He knew he shouldn't be — he knew Havana was one of the most fascinating cities in the world, but he had walked his socks off and done everything the guidebook recommended and now he'd had enough of sightseeing — on his own.

It would have been different if Pippa had been here. He put down the mojito he'd been toying with for half an hour. The ice had melted and the drink was like a watery alcohol soup.

Their last conversation had played over and over in his mind like a stuck DVD and he wished he could stop it. He longed for something to distract him from his thoughts. Maybe someone in the busy lobby might interest his detective's keen sense of observation, honed after years in the police.

Pippa's shrill voice still invaded his thoughts — the way she'd paced up and down in front of him, the way she'd gripped her hair in her hands.

'The trouble with you, Mark, is you don't do anything but work. You think work, you breathe work. Work, work, work. On the few occasions when we're out you're always talking about it. Even when we go on holiday you'll be thinking about it.

'Fact is, Mark, that your darned criminal cases and your precious mates in the force are more important to you than I am.'

She'd got angrier and angrier, her voice shriller and louder. That was when she'd let it slip about her affair. When she'd broken down and told him it was all over between them.

She'd felt neglected, needed someone to pay her attention. She'd felt discarded and lonely.

When all he'd tried to do was earn

money to pay for her expensive tastes and her love of good clothes and expensive perfume!

She was leaving. She'd found herself someone else, with a bigger bank balance. After ten years it had come to nothing. She wouldn't be back.

And here he was. On his own.

Mark knew he shouldn't have come here, he should have cancelled. But his boss wouldn't hear of it.

'Take the time out, Mark. Detective sergeants with marital problems make rotten policemen. Use this holiday to get your head in order and get yourself fully sorted. And don't come back until you've stopped brooding, and you're a hundred percent. That's an order.'

Had it done the trick? Here he was, in this place of sugar cane and trade winds, of beaches and coffee-coloured beauties, and his mind was still 4,500 miles away. And he was still brooding.

Mark raised his gaze from the floor. Something caught his attention. A minor ruckus over by Reception.

An English woman with shoulder-length hair curling uncontrollably in the humidity. Slim but curvy, too heavily clothed for the hot weather, skin still winter pale and untouched by the sun's rays. A new arrival.

She was clearly panicking and calling to a young girl of maybe eighteen or nineteen, who hadn't noticed the other woman's problems since she was talking animatedly to a young man who had engaged her in conversation.

It was in Mark's nature to sort things. He never could sit back and do nothing. He pulled his six-foot two frame out of the chair and ambled over.

The daughter — for the family resemblance was unmistakable — was glowingly attractive, a small neat nose like her mother's, peppered with freckles, her eyes lively. The only difference was the colour of their hair. The daughter's was still baby blonde.

Mark wished he and Pippa had been able to have children. He would have burst with pride to be able to boast a daughter like that. A child would have been something to cling on to when she'd left.

It was going to be a shame to interrupt what seemed to be the teenager's excellent attempt at speaking German to the young man, who laughed loudly at a shared joke. The young had that wonderful ability to live completely in the moment. They had no history of broken relationships, of shattered dreams to haul them into the past, or hopes for things that might be, to project them into an uncertain future.

They lived just for the here and now.

Mark would have stayed out of it but there was something about the small tableau which troubled his detective's eye. Something he had half seen but wasn't sure of, something he wanted to check.

Mark gently touched the girl's arm.

'I think your mother needs help.'

Immediately the girl dropped her

conversation. She stopped mid-sentence and turned away from the young man as surely as if he had donned a cloak of invisibility and disappeared.

A guilty flush rose in her cheeks as if she knew her parent needed looking after and that she had taken her eye off the ball.

There was a family dynamic going on there, deep layers of need, and Mark wondered what it was that they shared which meant they needed each other, but also, perhaps, desperately needed to break free of their bonds.

'Are you OK, Mum? Are you all right? Has anything happened?'

'It's my passport, I can't find it.' The note of panic in the woman's voice cut through the air.

'You put it in your moneybelt, Mum, under all those clothes. It's just like when you search for your glasses and find them on your head.'

The girl's voice was soothing, if frustrated. The two of them had forgotten Mark; they were wrapped in each other's worlds. It was obviously a well-worn pattern, this need to work together to resolve a crisis, one supporting the other.

Mark wandered away. He should leave them to it, not get involved. He was meant to be on holiday.

He wasn't meant to be tangling himself up in other people's complicated, precarious lives. He wasn't at work now, this was meant to be downtime.

He distracted himself by studying a revolving stand full of maps and postcards. It wasn't holding his interest.

Instead, the thing he had only suspected earlier he became more sure of, and it worried him. Once a detective, always a detective. His mind, constantly analysing, wouldn't leave things alone.

Mark picked up a street map, peering at it, seemingly intent on studying the best one to buy. But out of the corner of his eye to his right, he saw a man, stout, with a beer belly and a clipped beard dappling his chin.

The man held up his phone as if he was trying to shield it from a sunny window. In fact, Mark could have sworn he was taking photos of the Englishwoman and her daughter.

Photo after photo.

Mark turned his head a fraction to see if there was something noteworthy the man might be interested in above the reception desk. A painting, maybe, or a poem or saying by Che Guevara in an ornate plaque which might have caught a tourist's eye. People on holiday snapped the most mundane things.

But there was nothing, just blank marbled walls.

Mark turned back to study the stranger. He would even have gone over and confronted him, asked him in a pointed way if he could help him. But, like a magician disappearing in a puff of smoke, the man had gone, disappeared and melded into the midday crowds.

Not only had Mark failed to keep track of the man, but the mother and daughter had wandered off. Still, the Cuban heat hadn't robbed Mark of all his powers of detection.

As the two women, hooked arm in arm, trailed after the bellboy away across the lobby, Mark approached the desk and handed the girl a large denomination note.

'Can you please let me have some change in Cuban convertibles?' The receptionist turned her back to unlock a cash box behind the counter, and started counting out change.

Luckily, she gave Mark just enough time to tilt his head and scan the form she was processing. In a bold hand Mark read the names,

Mrs Bryony Kemp, Miss Anna Kemp.

He wondered where Mr Kemp was and why on earth he wasn't accompanying those two beautiful but somewhat vulnerable women, and when he might appear.

Sweet Sorrow

'What do you want to do on our first evening?' Bryony asked as they unpacked their cases.

White cargo pants and pastel coloured shorts for the day, swirly knee length dresses in bright colours for lunchtime outings and long sleeveless dresses with shoulder wraps for the evening. They had been told that Cuba was a place with virtually nothing to buy. No swanky shops, no street markets bursting with multiple stalls, no rows of colourful T-shirts and ranges of jeans, no strappy holiday dresses in floaty materials designed to empty the purses of tourists.

This was still a communist country that eschewed the capitalist hobby of shopping for new things you didn't need. What was more, the blockade of goods coming in meant that there was hardly any of the ubiquitous 'stuff' around that tempted holidaymakers and shoppers.

Everything the Cubans had, and that was very little, was used and used again.

As they had driven here in the taxi, Bryony had noticed radios, TVs, irons, electric lights and hoovers in little repair shops. It didn't seem to matter how old they were, they were obviously passed from generations and traded amongst friends and family.

They were repaired and remodelled until the last bit of life was extracted out of them and then, when they finally seemed dead, some brighter, sparkier engineer than the others would take them and bring them back into service again, using all the bits and parts to make something new.

Nothing was wasted and there was virtually nothing to buy. Bryony and Anna had been told that toothpaste and nice soap was difficult to get hold of.

They'd also been told that it was a

common thing for guests in hotels, at the end of their stay, to give a helpful chambermaid a bag full of clothes or items they no longer had a great need for. This was a thank-you to help this silent army of hard-working women get on in life.

Bryony, when she had heard this, welcomed the chance to bring all the clothes which had meant so much to her during her life with Warren. This would be their last outing, their swansong.

Her suitcase when she left this curious island would be lighter — not just of clothes but of memories.

This was her chance to cleanse herself, to drop the chains of memory, to release herself of the burden of things which once were part of her life but which would never be again.

She knew it would be painful saying goodbye to clothes which had been like friends in good times, but she must do it. She must at some point let go.

Bryony hung up the dress she used to

wear on the rare occasions when she and Warren had splashed out on tickets to the Royal Opera House. She had also worn it for anniversaries and special birthdays.

As she unfolded the dress and hung it on a hanger, she ran her hands over its thin cream and flesh-coloured silk, so soft, like the touch of a loved one's hand.

She remembered how Warren, unbidden and unasked, would take the ribbon strap which would work its way off her shoulder, and place it back in its rightful place, before giving her shoulder a squeeze.

Tears stung the back of her eyes and she fought to keep them from flowing.

As Anna scurried about, hanging up her own things, Bryony took a deep breath.

'These were my special trousers for when Dad and I were learning Argentine tango. Do you remember how we showed you our first moves and tripped on the carpet and nearly came a cropper?' Bryony laughed and then remembered how lovely it had been when they'd had dozens of lessons and had finally achieved their aim of being good dancers.

The trousers were split from ankle to calf. Bryony remembered how she would curl her ankle up and round Warren's knee when they performed a sensuous *ocho*.

She tucked the trousers away in the wardrobe, the memories were almost too painful. Then she put her special geometric patterned blouse on a hanger.

'Remember Dad's face the Christmas he gave this to me? He was so worried I might not like it but he was wrong. I've worn it so much, I've had to sew the buttons back on three times!'

'Are you sure you want to leave all those behind when you go, Mum? Won't you miss them?'

'In a way, love. But in another way, I need to be free of them. I won't be casting them off, and I won't be forgetting your Dad for ever. I'll be giving them a new home. The maids here will cherish them, they'll be of far more use to them than if I'd given them to a charity shop.

'Most of the Cuban chambermaids are young,' Bryony added. 'They'll wear my things to parade down the Malecón; they'll wear them on their first dates with their future husbands. My clothes, with their connections to a past life and to a much-loved marriage, will find a new life. They'll be better with these hardworking ladies in this beautiful sunny island that your father loved.

'My old memories will help those girls to make new memories, and help me to make a new life. I'm not forgetting your dad, just understanding that I need to move on.'

The last piece Bryony put in the wardrobe was a light cashmere stole in a silver grey which went with everything.

As she felt the softness in her hands, it brought back the time she and

Warren had escaped for a romantic weekend in Cornwall.

The stole had been warming her shoulders when they had spotted their first glow worm hiding in the grass verge on the road out of Polperro.

Warren had explained how the glow came about, that it was bioluminescence and she had marvelled about her husband's capacity to know something about everything.

You never needed an encyclopedia when you were with Warren.

Would she ever find a man like that again? She doubted it. He was one in a million.

A Welcome Change

Once all their unpacking was done, Bryony and Anna decided to go out, without any particular plan for the evening.

'Let's just wander, see where that gorgeous Caribbean wind takes us.'

The doorman opened the glass doors on to the street. The palm fronds waved and they stepped into air as warm as soup.

'I thought you had a list of salsa bars you wanted to visit,' Bryony said.

'I do.'

Anna tossed her hair in the breeze.

'But what I'm really looking forward to is an adventure. My life was so structured at school, I felt suffocated during my A-levels. I just want to go and float around.

'It'll be better at uni, and I'll love studying fine art but it'll still be work.

I've had my head stuck in books all year. Now we're on holiday.

'It's nice not having a timetable. A land like Cuba is full of possibilities and because it's reputedly so safe we've got nothing to worry about.'

Bryony found her hand clenching tightly over her handbag. She knew Anna worked incredibly hard at her studies.

She'd been praised by her teachers for being relentless in her A-level research, burning the midnight oil while other students tended to party.

Bryony wanted Anna to have fun but she'd had to be so in control without Warren by her side she found it impossible to let go.

Interrupting her thoughts, a Cuban youth with blue eyes and the deepest golden skin careered to a halt behind them. He jumped off the taxi bicycle he was riding, tatty but charming with a little roof and two seats for passengers.

'Engleesh, you Engleesh?'

'Yes.'

'I take you see the city. Best tour, very cheap. Show you everything, just one hour.'

'I don't think so.'

'Oh, Mum, let's. It'll be fine, don't worry.'

'That bike thing doesn't look safe — there are bits hanging off it.'

'But they all look like that. I'm sure it'll be OK.'

'My name is Norelvis. You know, like Elvis who sing the songs. I live in Havana since my birth, no-one knows it better. Come, I am strong, I will show you.'

The boy, who was in his late teens, continued to try to persuade them.

The way he cocked his head and dusted off the seats with a clean cloth was very appealing.

A number of flags flew from his handlebars, Canadian, French, the Union Jack. The poor boy was doing everything possible to appeal to all the tourists. Making a living here must be hard.

Bryony hesitated, but Anna grasped

her hand and pulled her gently towards the rickety vehicle.

'We'll agree the price before we go. Please, let's take a chance.'

They climbed in and as they bumped and rocked along the streets, with him pedalling like fury, Bryony started to enjoy the cool wind in her face and his knowledgeable commentary.

When she worked out in her head how little they were paying, she realised he was working hard for his money and she had to admire him.

'Here is the Museum of the Revolution,' he told them. 'Many photos of Che Guevara. It was former palace of *Il Presidente*. Inside is all mirrors, very pretty.'

When he said this, he couldn't help looking back at Anna.

'You feel OK, yes?' he asked. 'Please hold tight, be safe, pretty ladies.'

They continued down the Malecón, returning through backstreets.

He pedalled past near-derelict buildings, which at one time would have been very grand but were now falling apart, yet the strings of clean washing strung on ornate iron balconies showed people were still living in them.

Norelvis kept going past piles of rubble where obviously bits of the old masonry still fell down into the streets.

'We love all visitors,' he told them as local people waved whilst they drove past. 'Tourist money pays schools to teach men how to fix the old buildings. It is special scheme, very successful, helps tourist fund buildings they love to see.'

As they came to a part where restoration was taking place he stopped.

'Please, ladies, to get off. We show you beautiful old Cuban building.'

Some workmen, all obviously friends, greeted him warmly and proudly showed off the carpentry and work they were undertaking.

Where the buildings had been redecorated they were resplendent. In the last light of the day their ice-cream colours glowed — peppermint, cream, and very beautiful.

But right next door to a restored building there was a completely dilapidated one, with plants growing out of the guttering and a roof through which you could see the sky.

Bryony was amazed when a young woman with a carrier bag, coming back from work, walked in and went upstairs. This crumbling wreck was clearly her home.

It struck Bryony forcibly how much she had, and how little these people had, and yet they were all smiling and happy.

Bryony and Anna got back into the taxi bike and enjoyed just being ferried around. It gave them an idea of the lie of the city and how their hotel was positioned in relation to the tourist spots and the more out of the way backstreets.

After an hour, Norelvis turned to them and smiled.

'If you like to go for drink, I drop you off at good bar next to hotel. The best and much cheaper than hotel.'

They agreed, and he installed them at the best spot to watch the world go by, with a Cristal beer at a table under an awning.

'This is my card,' he said, bowing. 'Remember my name, Norelvis. I am every day at the hotel. Any time you need me, anywhere you want to go, I take you. Best prices.'

The boy's last wave and smile was just for Anna.

'Well, he was sweet,' Bryony said, tucking his card into her purse.

She would definitely use him again.

'Wasn't he? And so good-looking. I've never seen eyes that blue.'

It was the first spark of interest Anna had shown in boys for ages. She had been too buried in her studies.

What was more, Bryony tried not to stare as Anna absentmindedly popped peanuts into her mouth from the bowl of bar snacks on the table.

Amazingly, her daughter was eating without examining and questioning every mouthful.

Anorexia hadn't been mentioned by the doctor, but the food fads Anna had developed after Warren's death and her gradual but steady weight loss had worried Bryony to distraction.

She had noticed Anna suddenly developing an interest in cooking food but not in eating it. She had taken to carrying out huge baking sessions, making three or four cakes at a time and taking them in to her friends at school, or as presents for the teachers.

But she never had a slice herself.

For her daughter's lunch, Bryony would pack Anna a sandwich, a cereal bar and piece of fruit, but the lunch box would come back with only a few bites taken out of them.

When Bryony remarked on it, the lunch boxes started coming back empty but then Bryony suspected that Anna was just giving her food away.

At dinner in the evenings, watching Anna push food round her plate then cross her knife and fork with only a quarter having gone was so worrying.

But Bryony tried never to make a fuss. That only seemed to make Anna retreat more into herself.

Seeing Anna tuck into the peanuts without thinking was such a welcome change.

Maybe Cuba was going to unlock something good for both of them, Bryony thought as they wandered back to the hotel tired and ready for bed.

Desperate Panic

The next day was spent walking for miles. For the first time in a while, Anna had exclaimed that she was hungry mid-morning and had even agreed to having a coconut-flavoured ice-cream.

They had fun discovering the museum of rum, a homage to the nation's favourite drink.

They pondered over rows and rows of cigars of all different sizes, some sold in very expensive humidors for real connoisseurs. They bought a couple to take back home as presents and were given special little wooden boxes to protect them.

They marvelled at the lack of shops and at the friendliness of people standing with rickety handcarts in the backstreets, selling pineapples, guavas and plantains which looked like huge green bananas.

Then Norelvis, on his rickety taxi bike, spotted them. Bryony was pleased as her feet were killing her from all the walking.

It didn't take much for him to persuade them to hire him to go to see the Hotel Nacional. In its special garden, on manicured lawns, they sat at metal tables, drank tequila and made out they were there in its heyday, when Frank Sinatra and Ernest Hemingway had enjoyed the good life, and gambling and womanising were the main pursuits of visitors to the hotel.

When they had been revived with cocktails they set off again into the centre of Havana.

Everywhere they went, as they wandered the streets, Cuban boys would tell Anna how beautiful she was.

Bryony could almost see her daughter's self doubt beginning to fade a little, and Anna, forgetting her teenage gawkiness, almost beginning to believe their many compliments.

After their first proper day, they agreed that coming to Havana had been a good decision. In a couple of days they felt they had thoroughly come to know and love the city.

Other guests in the hotel had become familiar, like the group of young Canadians on a wedding party who took Anna under their wing and invited her to join them for drinks.

'Your accent is soooo cool; we could listen to you all day,' one of the girls told her.

While breakfasting or having coffee in the bar of the hotel, Bryony and Anna often saw the man with the pot belly and the small beard on his chin. He would smile enigmatically and do his strange little bow to them whenever their paths crossed.

'That man seems to be everywhere,' Bryony commented one day when they walked through the lobby after breakfast. 'Have you noticed him hanging around, Anna?'

'A bit.' Anna seemed unconcerned. 'Some people don't venture far from their hotels, do they? It's the hotel experience they come for, not to see the city. Besides, I've seen him on the odd occasion with an elderly woman with a walking-stick, maybe his mother or an aunt. I guess he's looking after her and can't move far off. He's probably bored.'

Anna was distracted and looking in her guidebook.

'Let's go for lunch tomorrow to that square where they have the bookstalls. I don't think there'll be much I want to buy — it's probably mostly dog-eared copies of Fidel Castro and Che Guevara's political pronouncements. But I'd like to browse. Some of the books are really old. They have artists selling paintings, too. And there's a great restaurant which does lobster kebabs.'

So it was settled and at noon the next day, they hailed Norelvis who'd become a firm friend and set off.

* * *

The following day, the weather had turned. In the morning it had lured them out with clear promising brightness but by lunchtime the sun had been forced away by broody grey clouds.

Bryony and Anna still sat outside at a nearby restaurant to enjoy the light and the heat, and chose a table under an awning, in case rain arrived.

They wanted to listen to the groups of musicians who everywhere plied their trade on the streets. 'Guantanamera' was the tune they all knew and played at the drop of a hat.

A white dog came to shelter under their table as, sure enough, the rain arrived in single fat raindrops that had started to splat on the pavement.

'Look, Mum, isn't he lovely? So fluffy. Wait, he's got a card around his neck.'

Anna leaned down and examined it, while she secretly slipped him a morsel of food.

'It says he's a street dog but he's looked after by some animal sanctuary. He's gorgeous, I wish we could take him back home with us.'

They debated what to do that afternoon and decided as the weather was inclement, they would pass the time in their room reading.

'I could do with a rest from all the sightseeing anyway,' Anna said, 'and I'm getting into my book. It's a murder story and I'm sure I know who did it but it's getting to the interesting bit.'

As lunch was being cleared away, Bryony stood up.

'I'll just nip inside to the loo before we go.'

She left Anna feeding the grateful dog surreptitiously under the table, enjoying his company.

On her way back Bryony walked across the inside dining-room which was a plant-filled atrium. She marvelled how, in this modern city, they actually kept their own chickens for eggs and these were left to wander. The birds

41

pecked around for crumbs under the table.

She had read that Cuba still found it difficult to get supplies of everyday goods, even common foodstuffs that we took for granted, so people kept chickens and grew their own vegetables, even on the balconies of high rise flats.

Emerging outside, Bryony scanned the tables looking for Anna's blonde hair amongst the Cubans' darker heads. She suddenly felt disorientated. They had been among a whole row of restaurants and all the tables looked the same.

People had finished their meals and gone, others had arrived for drinks. The landscape had changed. But look as she might, Bryony could not spot her daughter.

Anywhere.

You will not panic, she told herself, her subconscious lecturing her even as she felt her blood pressure start to rise.

Bryony hated the way that, since Warren had died, she was so acutely aware of the difference to one's life that a single minute could make. It was as though she was always ready for tragedy to strike. She knew that wasn't rational, but when you had been told your husband had suddenly gone for ever, it was difficult not to live life on a knife edge, to a certain extent.

Her inner voice kicked in. She'd had to do a lot of self-counselling since she'd lost Warren. Anna had probably just popped to the loo herself, or got talking with someone, she tried to convince herself.

Bryony made her way between the tables, trying to remember exactly where they had been sitting. Then, she saw the white dog underneath the table — their table. And on the table was a napkin with writing on.

A flood of relief rushed through her veins. Anna had left her a message. Of course, that was it. She'd popped off to browse the books, or view the paintings and she'd left a message to say she'd be back.

Bryony was pressing her hand to her chest, feeling as though her heart was going to jump out with all the anxiety.

There, on the stark white napkin in Anna's childish script with its loops and curls were words.

Mum, I'm just going . . .

The message ended mid-sentence.

Where?

To do what?

With whom?

Bryony's palms began to sweat. She walked out into the street, trying to remain calm. Her feet suddenly felt like lead as she paced up and down, searching the alleyways.

It was no good, she was running around like a crazy woman, alone in her distress. Unaccountably, Anna had disappeared.

Anxiety, which had been Bryony's constant companion since Warren had died and which she'd pushed away through sheer strength of will, forced itself back to sit firmly by her side.

The anxiety felt so close it could have

had its hands wrapped tightly round her throat, its mouth breathing on her cheek, making her shiver.

She ran back into the restaurant and grabbed the waitress by the arm.

'Did you see my daughter? She was sitting right here? Where did she go?'

The girl's English was almost non-existent. She shrugged her shoulders and turned her back, having no idea what this strange foreigner was going on about.

A huge wave of panic welled up from Bryony's stomach making her feel physically sick. It was as though she had fallen down a black hole. Where was the one person who was the dearest thing on earth to her?

All her worries about losing money and cameras and passports were nothing to this. Anna was what mattered, the only thing that mattered. Bryony knew how frail mere flesh and blood was.

She looked around for a policeman. There wasn't one. She started walking, then running, back to the hotel. She knew how people could be here one minute, gone the next. She couldn't lose another.

Please God, she prayed, don't let me lose another.

A Glimmer & Hope

When Bryony reached the hotel, she was distraught. She couldn't get a signal on her mobile so she couldn't try Anna's number or ring the police.

She looked for a phone box to call the police and couldn't find one. Even if she could, she didn't know how it worked, or what money to put in. Besides, she was shaking so much, she wouldn't even have been able to put the coins in the slot.

Finally, she saw the reception manager. He was kind and understanding, called the police and persuaded Bryony to sit down with some iced water.

They interviewed her in a side room, away from the hustle and bustle of reception.

The policeman took the whole thing in with a very South American air although he spoke perfect English.

The way he curled his lip at her seemed to indicate he thought she was just another highly-strung English tourist panicking over nothing.

'Cuba, madam, is the safest country in the Caribbean. Now, if you had gone to one of the other islands you might have had cause to worry. But here, we are carefully regulated, we value our tourist trade.'

He picked at his fingernail, looking supremely disinterested in the whole episode, as if he'd been here many times before.

'Your daughter is young, she wants to go off with other young people. Maybe she met someone interesting, perhaps a young man and has escaped on her own for a bit. She will be back.'

'You're wrong.'

You don't know our history, Bryony thought inwardly. We're not like any other mother and daughter. We protect each other, we have to. We know what it's like to lose someone you love.

She tried to stay calm, to moderate her voice.

'Anna would never go off on her own without telling me. She knows how worried I get.'

'Perhaps it is because you get so worried that she might want some of her own space.'

He looked at his watch, clearly anxious to get away.

'We will keep looking for her and will contact the hotel as soon as we have any news. Why don't you go and get off to bed? It is late.'

Bryony felt helpless and as if she had been talked to like a child.

* * *

That night was a restless sleep-deprived one for Bryony. Every hour she woke and checked her phone for messages.

She had informed the British Embassy in Havana, but although they had liaised with police, the clear message was that Bryony would simply

49

have to wait for developments.

She forced herself to go down for breakfast but despite going through the motions and collecting a plate of food from the buffet, she couldn't get down more than a glass of orange juice.

'Good morning.'

Bryony barely heard the deep-barrelled voice when it spoke, so lost was she in her own despair.

She looked up to see, standing in front of her, an Englishman who looked vaguely familiar. She mentally shuffled through the many faces in her head she had seen since arriving in Cuba.

Finally it came to her. He'd been in the lobby the first day they arrived, when she'd mislaid her passport.

She was so relieved to see a familiar face in amongst all these strangers, she had the urge then and there to pull him down to sit with her.

'Good morning,' Bryony said. 'I'm sorry, I forgot to thank you the other day when you helped us.'

'Are you all right, you look very pale?'

She was so grateful when, without asking, the stranger sat down opposite her, his broad frame filling the empty space at her table.

'Isn't your daughter joining you for breakfast today? Is she unwell?'

It was a total relief to have someone in front of her to talk to, someone whose eyes betrayed concern for her. Someone who spoke English.

Without even thinking, it all came pouring out. Bryony couldn't stop herself. She was so wound up with sleeplessness and worry and although it wasn't fair to unburden herself on this man she didn't have anyone else.

She'd phoned people at home last night, told all her friends and family. They'd fired suggestions at her and given their sympathies for her predicament, but what could they do from so far away?

Besides, they had their own busy lives, and Bryony had discovered, after losing Warren, that bereavement was a curious thing.

When you first lost a husband people were full of concern, they made real efforts to offer a shoulder to cry on. She even had wonderful neighbours who had cooked meals and brought them round.

But gradually, of course, people's own lives crowd in and take up their space. Because they see you around with a smile on your face and a purposeful gait they assume you're coping well.

What they don't see is the crumbling mass inside of you, the grief which permeates each day, sneaking up on you when you least expect it.

A song heard, a phrase said, even the back of someone's head in the street who you think you recognise as your beloved husband, and then suddenly realise that, of course, that's not possible. The departed simply exist in our heads and our hearts.

The bereaved had all this to contend

with and more, she had learned from bitter experience.

The man leaned forward, his chin balanced on his hands, listening to her intently.

How different from the Cuban policeman who had fidgeted and looked out of the window, who had made encouraging noises but who barely seemed to be listening.

'And you say that it is very out of character for your daughter to go off on her own?'

'Absolutely. You see . . . '

Bryony looked down. She'd come here to escape Warren's untimely death, not to have to explain it all again, yet she did, everything.

She recounted Warren's journey to hospital, her shock at his passing. And it felt good to get it off her chest.

'So, you see, Anna and I have become a tight knit unit. I look after her and she looks after me. She's always concerned for my welfare and she'd know that flitting off without an explanation would drive me demented.

'Something's happened to her, I just know it.'

Bryony wrung her hands, feeling entirely helpless.

It was only when the man, who had introduced himself as Sergeant Mark Greenstreet, explained that he was a policeman that Bryony felt a glimmer of hope in her grim situation.

Plan of Action

Mark Greenstreet's chin was set in a determined line. Bryony noticed he didn't smile much, but focused on every word she said.

He was a listener.

'Then we need to do something about it, don't we?' he said. 'The first twenty-four hours of a disappearance are the most important in determining whether someone will be found. I'll get myself a bit of breakfast, and you can give me some background.

'I want to know everything about your daughter, exactly where you were when you last saw her and anything strange or untoward that has happened to you since you arrived here. Then we can go out and start looking.'

While he made his way through an impossibly large plate of bacon, eggs and toast, Bryony couldn't help comparing and contrasting him to Warren.

Warren had worked in IT, had been a slightly-built man with a studious air about him. Jeans and T-shirts were the norm with him.

She only ever saw him in a suit when he was going to a job interview. His glasses, his slender figure and his relaxed style was what had attracted her to him.

Mark Greenstreet couldn't have been more his opposite — tall, broad and formal, wearing shirt and trousers, even while on holiday.

One thing was for certain, though. This man was full of energy.

Once he wiped his mouth with his serviette and polished off a third cup of coffee, he stood up briskly.

'Right, we'd better get going then.'

'But this is your holiday, I can't impose in that way. It's so wonderful of you to offer to help, but shouldn't you be out sightseeing?'

He gave her a hollow laugh and told

her briefly why he was here on his own. About his rift with his wife Pippa and how his hope they might put things back together looked now like a false hope.

Then he chuckled as he told her how bored he'd been.

'I have a very short attention span on holiday. I go crazy with nothing to do. It makes me feel useless. If I can be of some use to you then I'll have justified all this lazing about doing nothing.

'Anyway, sightseeing's no fun on your own — neither is sunbathing and sipping cocktails. Who can you laugh with? Who can you compare notes with about whether a pina colada is better than a mai tai?'

He rubbed his chin.

'One of the reasons I came to Cuba is that I wanted to brush up on my Spanish. When I was a student I ran a couple of holiday camps in South America for disabled kids. I learned a lot of Spanish there and I've always tried to keep it up. Maybe I can go with you and question some of the people at the restaurant. If we go there at lunchtime today, we might find diners who were there when Anna disappeared.'

For the first time since Anna had gone, Bryony felt the weight on her shoulders to be slightly lighter than before. Mark Greenstreet was such a decisive man, so sure of himself.

But then he would be, he'd worked on similar investigations before.

Bryony had noticed him on the odd occasion when she and Anna had been on their way out of the hotel. He was a good-looking guy. He'd always looked as if he'd been waiting for someone which, in some way, she now knew he had.

She knew how awful it was to lose your partner, and whether through bereavement or marital break-up, it still left you in limbo. She and Mark Greenstreet were two lost souls in this alien land.

When she got back to her room, her

hotel phone was ringing. She ran to pick it up.

'Hi, I'm so glad I caught you.'

It was Paul, Warren's brother. Bryony lay on the bed. It was good to hear a familiar voice.

She'd tried to get hold of Paul as soon as Anna disappeared but he was away working on a building site. Owning his own successful building company, he spent a lot of time travelling round England.

'This stuff with Anna sounds awful — is there anything I can do?'

Paul was always helpful, he'd been a rock and a comfort through her dark times.

It helped that he didn't look at all like Warren, although they were brothers. Paul was the sporty outdoors type whereas Warren had always had his head buried over a laptop.

'You could do something for me,' she said. 'I can't get a phone signal and the internet connection over here is hopeless, you can hardly ever get it and when you do it's as slow as a snail.

'Could you possibly go on to Anna's Facebook and Twitter accounts and see what activity there's been? Whether there are any clues to where she might have gone, or who she might have gone with.'

'I'd need her passwords and e-mail account details. Isn't that just a bit too much like snooping? If she has just maybe gone off with someone and slept on their sofa or floor, won't she be livid at you intruding?'

'I've thought of all that, Paul. In fact I churned it over in my mind endlessly last night. I have to do something, though, don't you see? If she turns up and she's angry with me then I'll have to live with it. I have her password details in my handbag. Let me go and get them for you.'

She retrieved the bit of paper and read him the details.

'Warren insisted she give us her passwords when we allowed her to become involved in any social networking. Being an IT geek, he knew the dangers as well as the benefits of having a virtual life. It was one of his many ways of protecting her.'

'OK, I'm happy to be of help. Look, Bryony, the job I'm working on at the moment is going fine. I've got a brilliant project manager who's keeping it all on track. I could come over, I could fly there right now.'

'Absolutely not. I couldn't pull you away from your work, I know how important it is to you. I have to sort this on my own.

'I'm sure I'm worrying unduly. Anna's like any teenager, she may just have gone off with some of the young Canadians at the hotel, they seem to like having fun.'

Bryony was trying to convince herself as much as her brother-in-law.

'I keep on trying to rationalise what's happened,' she continued. 'After all, she's eighteen, she's not a child any more and I wonder whether I've just been too much for her lately, trying to be superwoman and keep it all together.

'Maybe she needed a break from me, and maybe she'll just wander in any moment. To have you spend all that money and pull you away from your work for nothing would be ridiculous. Besides, I came over here to try to be more independent without Warren.'

'You don't have to be.'

The silence hung in the air like a fruit waiting to be picked. Bryony had an inkling of what Paul wanted to say. She had a feeling he'd been on the verge of trying to turn their relationship into more than just a bereaved sister-in-law and caring brother-in-law for some time.

It wasn't that she didn't like him, she did. A lot. But she wasn't ready for another relationship, she wasn't sure if she ever would be.

Besides, how weird would it seem to the family, and to Anna in particular, to find out that her mother had started a relationship with her uncle? Bryony couldn't go there. Her life needed fewer complications, not more.

As she spoke, she toyed with Anna's necklace which had been lying on the bedside cupboard between their beds. Warren had given it to Anna on her eighteenth birthday.

On the chain was a small silver globe with the continents engraved upon it. He'd urged his daughter to travel. She nearly always wore it, but she'd gone out without it the day she'd disappeared.

Was Anna maybe subconsciously trying to forget him?

Bryony closed her eyes and tried to remember Warren's face. But the image was cloudy after all this time, the edges fuzzy. She couldn't quite remember the angle of his nose, the tone of his skin.

At this point, she'd usually take out the photo of Warren she kept in her purse, his smiling happy face held next to hers, his hand stroking her cheek.

But she resisted. She mustn't keep looking back, and she mustn't keep resuscitating the memory of Warren to help her get through things.

'I'm fine, Paul. Besides, there is someone out here who's helping me. He's a policeman, on holiday. His other half couldn't make it, so he has time on his hands and he's offered to help investigate where Anna's got to. He speaks Spanish as well.

'I'm sorry, but I have to get ready. We're going off to the restaurant to quiz the people there. It's good, isn't it, that I've got someone to help me?'

There was silence at the other end of the phone, and a long pause before Paul spoke.

'Yes, of course. What's his name?'

'Mark, Mark Greenstreet. Let me know once you've had a look at Anna's Facebook and Twitter stuff, won't you?'

Bryony felt bad as she put the phone down. She knew Paul had reached the point in his life where he wanted a relationship.

He'd always envied Warren that and although when he was younger, the business had been enough for him, now he was successful, he had no-one to share his success with.

One Step at a Time

While Bryony was getting ready, she received a call from Mark.

'Do you have any photos handy of Anna?'

'Loads, only they're just on my phone.'

'That's good enough. I've spoken to the woman in the business centre here. I explained Anna's disappearance and she's happy to help by downloading her photo and printing a poster.

'She's going to write it in Spanish and put on both our mobile numbers in case people see her. She has a daughter the same age, and she remembered how pretty and how polite Anna was when she bought a phone card from her earlier in the week.

'We can fix the posters to trees round the hotel and ask the restaurant and bar owners to put them up in their cafés.

There might be some youth hostels and there's a university near there, too, where we can display it. If Anna's gone off, it's most likely with a group of young people.'

Bryony was only too pleased to be doing something practical.

The posters, when they were done, were brilliant, with a clear photo of Anna which would surely jog people's memory.

Bryony met Mark outside the hotel, clutching the set of posters in her handbag. He was already in earnest conversation with Norelvis.

The taxi bike was a bit too small for a man of Mark's height and he was apologising to the young lad that, today, they were going to take a taxi car.

Norelvis offered to take some of the posters and distribute them among all the local drivers. They saw everything that happened in Havana, they were like a bush telegraph.

'Which of the taxis has the best driver?' Mark asked Norelvis.

'This one, of course.'

The boy waved his hand and one of the old Fifties Oldsmobiles which the Cubans still used as taxis pulled up.

'Alfonso is my brother. He will take you wherever you need to go, and he knows everyone it is useful to know.'

The huge car was turquoise, with cherry-coloured leather seats. Alfonso dropped them off as near as he could to *Calle Mercaderes*, the cobbled pedestrianised street leading to the square where Anna had disappeared.

For Mark, all this activity was like a shot of adrenaline straight into the heart. He felt energised for the first time in ages.

His boss had sent him away to get his head together but all that the enforced rest of a holiday had done was to frustrate him. He had found it turned him in on himself and all that had gone wrong with Pippa and their relationship.

Mark had done his best to make that right, to turn it around, to try again, but she'd found someone else and told him her future no longer lay with him.

The desolation of losing everything he'd worked for, the thought of starting up again as a single man had threatened to destroy him.

These last few weeks, he'd even wondered how he would be able to concentrate on work. It was as though his whole life was crumbling around him.

But now, instead of all that stuff he couldn't do anything about, he had been thinking about Bryony Kemp, how strong she was and how unfair life was to throw her yet another difficulty.

★　★　★

Mark considered Bryony as they walked down the *Calle Mercarderes*. She was determined, like a she-tiger looking for its cub.

Local Habaneros looked at her curiously as they sat on their steps chatting, or rearranging the pineapples, bananas and guavas they sold for a few Cuban convertible pesos from hand-carts on the streets.

It was as if they were wondering why an Englishwoman wasn't doing the usual tourist loitering, observing the 18th-century buildings and taking photos.

'You don't have to go so fast,' Mark urged her. 'Let's have a coffee, talk about what we're doing here, who we're going to see.'

'What's the point in that?'

Bryony's dark eyes were flashing with intensity, with the need to get things done, with barely disguised fear for her lost only child.

He grasped her by the shoulders and stopped her dead in her tracks.

'Listen to me, Bryony. I've seen parents in a similar state when I've carried out investigations before. There are two types. There are those who simply crumble and spend hours staring into space or take to their beds.

'Then there are the doers, those

parents who have to get out and do something positive, who have to search all day and all night long if necessary until they're exhausted. You must slow down if you're to survive this.'

He sighed.

'I know you feel you have to get out and do everything at once, but one of the keys to detection is cool, quiet, thinking and working stuff through. It's observing and talking to people, and digesting what they tell you. It's not rushing about and sending yourself crazy in the process. If you do that, you miss things.

'I've seen cops, good cops, at the end of long investigations say, 'If only we'd seen that, it was right in front of our faces and we missed it'. That sort of regret comes from over-activity and not enough calm thought.'

He grasped her shoulders.

'We could even see stuff here, in this road, close to where Anna disappeared which might be vital to finding her. These things may not be immediately apparent but they might become important once we go on.

'All I'm saying, Bryony, is slow down, please.'

He could see the frustration in her eyes. He could sense the need not to be told what to do, as he felt her body rigid under his hands.

He saw her chest rise and fall.

'I . . . ' she bit her lip, the words not coming easily ' . . . need to stand up on my own two feet. I'm on my own now, you see. I don't have Warren to help or to confide in. You need to let me do things my way.'

He released her gently, as if she was a wounded cat he was trying to treat.

'What you need is to calm down and listen to an expert. I'm not lording it over you but believe me, I know what I'm doing. We will find Anna, we will.'

He nodded his head, long and hard.

'I have never had a missing persons investigation that I didn't solve. I've won commendations for my skills. But I will say this, no missing child was ever found by a bunch of people running around headstrong and worked up, rushing into things.'

For a moment, as her shoulders drooped, he thought she might burst into tears.

But it was almost as if Bryony Kemp had run out of tears to cry.

She closed her eyes, then opened them again.

'I'm sorry, you're right. We'll do it your way. But you must promise me we'll find her.'

'I promise,' Mark said, and suddenly this investigation meant more to him than any other he'd undertaken.

Because he knew that the woman standing in front of him couldn't take any more disappointments in life, or any more fear, or uncertainty.

She needed putting back together.

He knew what it was like, that feeling that everything had fallen apart and nothing could be right again.

He knew it and he hated it.

If it killed him, he was going to put

Bryony Kemp back together again. He was going to fix the chips and the breaks which she had suffered, make her whole.

And in doing so, perhaps, just perhaps, he might be able to find what was real, to forget his own wounded past, and to put himself back together again.

A Positive Lead?

Mark and Bryony walked in silence for the next few minutes, and she seemed to take his advice, looking carefully up at the wrought iron balconies and into the renovated blocks of flats as if the answer could be there somewhere. Some looked straight through to open courtyards streaming with sunshine.

Maybe the dark entrances to those old apartment blocks, cool with their mini-jungles of houseplants could hold all the secrets. Maybe Anna was in one of those somewhere — either as a willing guest, or an unwilling captive.

Mark wondered if he'd been too rough on Bryony.

There was an air of fragility surrounding her. The way she clung to her handbag like a lifebelt, her knuckles white as they gripped too tight.

The way her shoulders were up

again, tense. The way she clutched her jacket round her as if desperate for comfort.

Mark understood, he really did, what it must be like to lose a husband who had been a protector. But it also occurred to him that, although he'd met many women in the same position, women whose husbands had been lost in accidents, he had always been able to approach them in a detached professional way. It was his job.

Now, he wasn't working, and this woman and her disappeared daughter were more than simply people he was paid to help.

What's more, this was a strange country with different rules he didn't understand. He wondered for a fraction of a second whether he should be liaising with the Cuban police, then thought better of it. The last thing he needed was someone telling him what he could or couldn't do — or blocking his modus operandi.

This was still a communist country

with tough laws, and people still buttoned their lips if you tried to question authority, or the regime.

The sun beat down, barely tempered by the breeze in amongst the hot stone buildings.

'Let's put up some of these posters.'

He and Bryony attached posters to trees and lamp posts and curious people came up, looked and peered sympathetically at Bryony.

A few approached her and asked how old Anna was and where she had been last seen.

In the past, in Cuba under different regimes, people had disappeared. Memories here were long and people understood what it was like to have that empty hole in your life where a loved one had once been.

An old woman came up to Bryony, her forehead wrinkled with compassion and touched Bryony's arm to comfort her.

The old people had hearts which were etched with memories of a time when it wasn't unusual to lose a daughter or a son permanently and for no trace of them to be found. Ever.

This country had a painful past and an uneasy future. Their Russian allies had abandoned them when the USSR broke up. Their new ally was China, whilst they felt aggrieved that America still chose to turn its back on them. They had an uncomfortable past and an uncertain future.

'Come on,' Mark said. 'Let's go and have a word with the owner of the restaurant where you two had lunch. Los Pollos, that was its name, wasn't it?'

When they got there, the owner shook his head. He had seen nothing, having been busy sorting out a problem in the kitchen that day.

'The waitress who served you is in at noon. You have only half an hour to wait, talk to her by all means.'

'We'll come back,' Mark said. Then he turned to Bryony. 'Let's walk round the square and show people Anna's photo. Someone must remember her.'

A couple of people did; she was distinctive, young, blonde and pretty. She'd chatted to them about paintings.

One stall owner was particularly helpful. He had been selling a selection of expensive art works quite different from the others, not modern, but from the 19th and early 20th centuries.

He had a distinctive look, very clean cut, a perfectly tailored suit, trendy pointy-toed shoes and a sleek hairdo. The trade in early paintings was obviously lucrative.

He looked thoughtful.

'I do remember this young lady. She had a great interest in art and books. I saw her talking to a young man. I think he might have been a Canadian. I believe I saw her wander off that way, into one of those bars, I think.

'Those are the bars where all the tourists go, they think it is the real Havana but it is not. Nevertheless, they have fun. The young need to have fun while they can, before life bears down on them.' The scent of expensive aftershave exuded from him.

As they turned to go, the stall owner stopped them.

'Please, let us exchange telephone numbers. My name is Gustavo Jimenez. I have been trading here for many years; I know a lot of people. I will ask around and if anything turns up I will let you know. Do feel free to call me whenever you wish.'

He gave them a smile displaying perfect white teeth.

'Thank you, Mr Jimenez, you've been very helpful,' Mark said.

'Call me Gustavo, please.' He gave a small bow, watching them all the while.

'I guess Anna just got chatting to this Canadian Gustavo mentioned,' Bryony said as they walked away. 'Anna's always so friendly and sometimes she loses track of time when she's talking about art. What a helpful man.'

Bryony seemed comforted that they might be getting somewhere, but Mark had learned to keep up his guard.

'In fact, everyone's so helpful, I think that's one of the things that defines Cubans, don't you?' Bryony continued. 'They seem to have very little in the way of possessions. There are so few shops and one that Anna and I did go into had virtually nothing on the shelves.

'But their lack of things doesn't seem to bother them, they're so nice and so pleased to meet foreigners. It feels safe here, it gives me hope that Anna is OK.'

Mark nodded but Bryony was unsure of his expression. She guessed he had seen many difficult things in his policing and met many bad people but she tried not to think of that in connection with Anna.

She noticed as they made their way down the road, that Mark looked behind him more than once.

The two of them immediately made their way down to the bars Gustavo Jimenez had seen Anna walk into. They handed out their posters but not one person at that end of the square remembered Anna.

'That's curious,' Mark remarked as they headed back to the restaurant. 'It would have been busy round here, and lots of the locals hang around the same bars. It's odd to have just one sighting of someone in a place like this.'

'It feels a bit hopeless.' Bryony was starting to flag, her feet were aching and the bright optimism from this morning was beginning to dull.

'Let's go back to Los Pollos and see if the waitress has started her shift.'

* * *

She had. She was a young plump girl with the name of Theresa. She spoke so little English that Mark had to converse with her in Spanish.

'I'm impressed by your Spanish,' Bryony said.

'It's not that good but I get by.'

'What did she say?'

'Her shift finished just before the end of your meal. She's gone off to get the waiter who cleared the tables in case he noticed anything.'

While they waited, Mark started taking photos on his phone.

'It's always useful,' he explained, 'to take photos when you're carrying out an investigation. There are so many things you can miss, so many tiny points worth pondering. It really is true that a picture tells a thousand tales.'

They sat down to wait for the waiter who was busy with other customers. As Mark scrolled through the photos on his phone, Bryony glanced at them, too. As one appeared of an overweight man, with a goatee beard, she sat up.

'Oh, now who is that man? Do you know him, Mark?' Bryony asked. 'Now I think of it, I remember he seemed to be all over the hotel one way and another. We assumed it was because he was with an elderly relative.'

'So you noticed him, too.'

Mark went on to tell Bryony about what he had seen the day she had lost her passport. About the way the man with the beard seemed to be taking photos.

'It was a curious thing to do, but on holiday, people take photos of everything and nothing. At the time, I brushed it off as my imagination. I decided I'd spent too long being a detective and should relax more while I was on holiday. I'd all but forgotten him but now, I think I might have been right. Maybe he was interested in you and Anna for some reason.'

At that point, the waiter arrived. His English was much better than the waitress's. He glanced at the photo they were looking at.

'Do you want to know who this man is?' he asked.

'Why?' Mark exclaimed. 'Do you know him?'

'I do not know him, but I know of him. He exports cigars, he is a businessman. We do not have many such men in Cuba. Entrepreneurs are few and far between. You are looking for the young lady, the girl with the blonde hair, yes?'

'Yes!' Bryony sat up in her seat. 'She's my daughter. She's disappeared.'

'Well, I saw her with this man. She was speaking to him as I cleared your table. She was laughing with him, they shared a joke.'

'But where did they go, did you see where they went, did you hear what they were saying?'

Bryony's heart was beating like a drum as she bombarded him with questions. It was the first proper lead they'd had.

'I am sorry.' The waiter shrugged his shoulders. 'I was very busy, there were many tables to clear. I do not pay much attention to tourists and their talk, it is all about whether they have seen this museum or been to that art gallery. I have heard it all before and they all ask the same questions.

'We Cubans are always trying to sell the little we have, although I cannot think your daughter would have been in the market for this man's cigars.'

Mark frowned.

'You say you know of this man. But do you know his name?'

'No, but they will know of him at the cigar museum. This is a small city, and I believe he has donated things to the museum. You should ask there.'

Dangerous Territory

Mark and Bryony made their way down the streets of Old Havana until they reached the cigar museum, situated on the top floor of an old colonial house.

The scent of the hundreds of vintage and modern cigars displayed in elegant wooden and glass cabinets teased their noses. A smell of sweet, fresh tobacco.

An elegant woman stood behind the counter, her red dress contrasting with her deep coffee-coloured skin. Her dark hair was slicked back against her head.

'Would you like tickets for the museum?'

'Er, not today, thank you,' Mark said. 'We'll come back another time. We're actually looking to buy cigars.'

Bryony raised an eyebrow in his direction. That was news to her.

'We have a very good shop here in the museum.'

'Thank you, but I'm actually interested in buying in bulk, I want to ship them back to my shop in London.

'I understand there is a man locally who trades in cigars. He and I met the other night in the Plaza Vieja. He gave me a card with his address and telephone number but stupidly I lost it. I took a photo of him.'

'Ah.' Looking at the man in the photo, she now smiled at Mark as if he were an honoured guest. 'That is Mr Otto Weber, a German cigar exporter; he has lived here for years. I think I have one of his cards here, I can copy his address down for you. His house is next to the Society for the Preservation of Steam Locomotives of Cuba, you cannot miss it.'

'Thank you, you're very helpful.'

The address she gave him was in one of the leafy more exclusive parts of the city behind the Hotel Nacional. Once they were outside again in the heat of mid-afternoon, Mark turned to Bryony.

'I know you must be tired, but we

should go there now.'

'I'll never be so tired that I can't search for my daughter. If this man's got something to do with her disappearance we need to find him. But what on earth could he want with Anna? I can't believe she'd willingly go off with some middle-aged stranger. He must be up to no good, but why?'

'I have no idea.' Mark hailed one of the taxi bikes. 'But we must continue to look like tourists and not arouse any suspicion. That's why I pretended to the woman in the museum that I wanted to buy cigars. I don't want to alert this guy to the fact we're looking for him. This isn't my patch, so I'm like a fish out of water.

'Usually when I'm carrying out an investigation, I know something about how an area works, who its people are. I have something to go on. Here, it's all so different: the language, the people. But we'll get by. I promise you we'll find Anna, whatever we have to do.

'Now, take out your guidebook and

tell me what's near to where this guy lives. We're going to pose as tourists who have got lost and gone a bit off the beaten track, so we've got to look plausible. I don't know who this man is or why he had an interest in you or Anna, but no-one must suspect we're looking for her.'

When they handed the piece of paper with the address to the taxi bike driver, he gave them a curious look.

'Next to the Society for Steam Locomotives? I have never heard of this. No tourists go there, are you sure this is where you want? Do you not prefer to go to somewhere more interesting?'

'No,' Mark insisted, 'that is definitely the place we want to go.'

When they alighted from the taxi bike they stood across the road, away from Otto Weber's house.

Mark dragged Bryony over to a small patch of public garden opposite with a bench they could sit on, where they could observe the front door without being spotted. They had definitely discovered the right house.

The house next door had a highly polished brass plaque announcing the *Steam Locomotive Society of Cuba*. Next to that, Otto Weber's building was an old house with faded brickwork and ornate iron railings. Once very fine, it was now tatty and faded, like an old duchess past her prime. It wasn't large or opulent, a house owned by someone well off rather than very rich.

Mark studied the front of the house.

'All the windows are closed even on this baking hot day. It doesn't look to me like anyone's in,' Mark said.

'Should we just knock on the door?'

'It could be dangerous.'

This was the first time he had voiced any fears about them being in danger. Inwardly, Bryony could have hugged him at that moment. Those dark thoughts had been at the back of her consciousness, but his calm presence had pushed them away.

He had been focused and cool and it

was only now they were much nearer to finding out what might have happened to Anna that he was warning her, guiding her as to what they should do.

She could never have done this alone, and she strongly suspected that the Cuban police would have done nothing. They seemed to have assumed Anna had just launched off on her own, yet Bryony knew her daughter, and she knew their shared past.

Her daughter would never have done anything to cause Bryony worry. Something very bad must have happened.

In all the many months since Warren had died, Bryony had seen it as a matter of pride to cope and be independent. That was one of the reasons she hadn't let Paul, her brother-in-law, into her life, however much he'd hinted and cajoled.

She had been acutely aware that she could have used him as a crutch to support her in her grief, but she hadn't wanted to be dependent upon any man like she had been on Warren.

Gradually, after the initial shock of grief had passed, Bryony had come to realise that, perhaps, her husband being so capable, his taking charge of most things hadn't been the best thing for her. If he had survived, that wouldn't have been a problem, but relying totally on him had served her badly after his death.

Relying on another man so totally would be folly, she had come to realise. The loss if they went was too awful to contemplate.

She had wanted to be strong and she had managed to dig up reserves of strength she never knew she had. But the pressure had told on her, making her more anxious even when doing simple things.

She'd taken this holiday to force her out of her anxiety, to prove to herself she could take risks and triumph.

She surprised herself now, as she and Mark sat in the shade on the bench in this leafy spot. She felt . . . OK. Apprehensive, wondering what to do next, but she wasn't caving in. She felt empowered.

Coping with something like this would probably have cracked her up had it not been for Mark's calm presence. He was a powerful force but he was only telling her what to do because he was an expert.

He could have played the macho man and told her to go back to the hotel whilst he dealt with stuff. But instead, he'd taken her fully on board. She was a part of this as much as he was, and it felt good to be doing something and to be guided, not just led like a puppy on a lead.

They were working through this mystery together, and she was his equal partner.

A Waiting Game

Mark had clearly been thinking, all the while seeming to study the guidebook, while Bryony studied the house.

'Wait a minute.' Her voice was charged with excitement. 'There is someone inside. Look, it's a woman, opening the windows and wiping them down.'

'Brilliant, she must be his cleaner. Right, come with me, you're going to have to hone your acting skills while we find out a bit more about this Mr Otto Weber.'

It seemed to take a lifetime for the maid to answer the door, and when she did, she was very cautious, only opening it a fraction.

'So sorry to disturb you,' Mark said with a broad smile. 'We've been wandering for ages. We were looking for the art museum, we're sure it's round here somewhere but the street is so quiet there's no-one to ask.'

The maid's face softened a bit as Mark worked his magic on her. For the first time, Bryony realised that Mark had a lot of charm. It was just that most of the time he hid it behind a stern exterior.

The maid seemed to melt, as well she might. Mark had blessed her with a gentle smile and an open countenance, his grey eyes appealing and his forehead graced by the quirk of a questioning eyebrow.

The maid smiled at him.

'It is not far. You walk down here.' She opened the door further to point down the street.

As Bryony paid attention and nodded, she decided to ask more questions as she realised that this would give Mark the chance to peer into the house, taking in everything.

'Sorry,' Bryony said, 'I didn't quite catch that. Can you repeat it?'

'You go two blocks down, then you

go *a la derecha*, how you say?' She hesitated. 'I do not know . . . ' she pointed to the right ' . . . then three blocks and *a la izquierda*.'

'Ah, right, then left? OK, you're very helpful, thank you. And if we want the Museum of the Revolution, is that far? Could you show me on the map?' Bryony asked.

The woman peered at the map for a while then shook her head.

'I do not know, I do not think it is close to here. You will have to ask someone else.'

'Maybe the householder is in, perhaps they will know?' Mark suggested.

'No, he is not in. He is gone to the country. Sorry, I do not know. I must go now, I am busy.'

They let her shut the door then walked away.

There wasn't much more they could get out of the poor woman, and besides, she was busy. It would take a long time to clean a house that large.

'Come on,' Mark said, turning left

quickly once they were out of sight.

He grasped Bryony's hand and ran with her round the block, in a circle, to come out again on the corner where they could see Otto Weber's house again, but still be hidden.

'What do we do now?'

'Well, at least we know he's gone away. I don't want to frighten you, Bryony, but we have to face up to the fact that, for some reason, Otto Weber could have kidnapped Anna and taken her with him into the country.'

'Oh, good heavens, why would he do that, and how on earth will we ever find her if she's not in Havana any more?'

'There are ways,' Mark said. 'Look, I'm starving, and there was a woman selling home-made malanga fritters from a stall we just passed. Let's pick up a few of those and we'll wait here for a while and see if anything happens. I don't know what, but it's the best lead we've got.'

As they sat and munched the tasty

fried snacks, Bryony looked question-
ingly at Mark.

'Are we on a stake out?' she asked.

Mark smiled.

It was a terrific smile. Bryony hadn't
seen it much, and it suited him. He
should do it more often.

'Sort of. Loads of police work is just
watching and waiting. It's tedious but
you get used to it, and most of the time
it pays results.

'Back home, I'd have other resources.
I'd be checking CCTV cameras and
looking into people's backgrounds but
here, well, we've no option except just
the good old tactic of watch and wait.'

★　★　★

Wait they did, for a whole hour and a
half until the cleaning lady finally
emerged from the house carrying a
cloth bag slung over her shoulder and
in her other hand a bag of rubbish.

Cubans didn't produce much rubbish. With there being so few goods to

buy and a shortage of everything, including packaging, they made sure they re-used it all. Even the taxi bikes' little sunshades were often repaired with old cardboard boxes and finished off with plastic bags to keep out the rain.

Bryony had even noticed, when they'd been searching earlier, that someone had made a paper chain to decorate a doorway out of old newspapers. She'd had to admire the Cubans' resourcefulness.

There simply weren't the mountains of rubbish here in Havana that people produced back in England.

As the maid disappeared down the street, Mark sprung into action.

'Come on.'

He shot forward to the front door, grabbed the rubbish bag and walked as quickly as possible with it in the other direction.

As soon as he saw a cab back on the main road, he hailed it to take them to the Hotel Parque Central.

'Come on,' he said to Bryony, 'we need to sort this in private.'

★   ★   ★

When they reached the hotel, he took Bryony up to his room and emptied the rubbish bag on to the carpet.

Thankfully, it wasn't smelly rubbish, apart from a few orange peels. It was mainly papers.

Mark tossed stuff here and there, looking intently as he did so.

'What are you looking for?' Bryony asked.

'Anything. It's surprising how much information you can put together on people's lives from their rubbish. Ah, here we go.'

'What's that?'

'An envelope, addressed to Otto Weber, Pedro Plantation, Trinidad.'

He held it up with glee like an Olympian holding up a gold medal.

'That's all we need. We're going to Trinidad.'

'Trinidad? That's miles away, it'll cost a fortune.'

'No, not Trinidad and Tobago — this is Trinidad, Cuba.'

Mark leaned over and grabbed a map.

'Here.' He punched the spot. 'It's a long drive — about four or five hours — but it's certainly do-able.

'Trinidad is known as one of the older, more historical and well-preserved, towns in Cuba. It's small but it's quite lively. There's a music scene, salsa bars and suchlike, a few notable buildings, and it's not far from the coast.

'Outside it there are acres and acres of sugar and tobacco plantations, little farms and deserted countryside. It's the perfect place to hide someone if you wanted to get them out of the way for some reason.'

'But what reason?'

'Who knows? But if you're up for it, so am I. It might be the only way we're going to find Anna. Why don't you go

102

and pack an overnight bag and I'll see you in the foyer in an hour.'

'Let's do it.'

For the first time since this whole mystery started, Bryony felt a chink of hope.

The two of them raised their hands in a high five.

'See you in a bit,' Bryony said. 'And by the way, thank you, Mark. Thank you so much, for being here and for taking this seriously. Well, just for doing something to help.'

'It's nothing,' he said, and that old gruff exterior returned.

He just didn't know how much of a hero he was turning out to be.

Clinging to Hope

They met an hour later. Bryony had to look for Mark. He wasn't sitting in the foyer doing nothing, but was outside the front of the hotel, on the Paseo de Marti. Mark was in deep conversation with Norelvis, who looked excited and energised, and his brother, Alfonso, who looked stern, more like a father than a brother.

'I am only lending you my taxi because I think I can trust you with these people.' Alfonso was looking Norelvis straight in the eye. 'Not only that, it will make us a good wage to bring back to our mother. But you be careful. That taxi is my livelihood, treat it well.'

Norelvis patted Alfonso on his bulging tummy.

'And you look after the taxi bike. Riding it instead of sitting in this taxi of yours, you will get fit and lose some fat. It will do us both good, yes?'

'Just remember me when I am old, my brother, and remember this opportunity I am giving you.'

Norelvis looked as proud as punch as he loaded Mark's small suitcase and Bryony's overnight bag into the Oldsmobile.

'So you're driving, Norelvis?' Bryony said apprehensively.

He looked very young, in her mind, to be taking charge of such a fine and beautifully preserved car.

'I am good driver. And with this practice I will get better and better.' He took her hand earnestly. 'Also, I want to find your Anna. She is very beautiful. Wherever she has gone we must find her, yes?'

'Yes.'

Bryony felt a tear come to her eye at the concern of this young man and his willingness to give them his time.

'Mr Mark says we will find her,' Norelvis said, 'and with me coming to help you two with the languages and driving like a very good chauffeur, we will find her. We will bring her back and we will punish very hard the people who have taken her.'

Bryony handed him her suitcase and climbed on to the baking-hot leather seat next to Mark. Buoyed by their optimism, her heart was full of confidence and she was delighted at last to be doing something to get her dearest Anna back.

As soon as she relaxed into the leather seats and the big old car growled away into Havana's traffic, the questions started flooding into her head.

Had Anna really been taken by this man Otto Weber, and if so, why? She didn't even like to think of all the possible answers to that question.

Or, were they going off on some wild goose chase, only to leave Anna here back in Havana, lost somewhere? Could she have had an accident and be lying in some hospital somewhere?

But the Cuban police had checked all that and they or the Embassy would have found her if that was the case.

Bryony had reported into Reception to see if there were any messages and there was only one, telling her the search was still ongoing.

Most of all, if Anna had been taken by the German man, by this Otto Weber, would they get there on time before he did her real harm?

★   ★   ★

As the Oldsmobile careered out of Havana Vieja, the road became more of a speeding highway. Mark was glad it was Norelvis who was driving and not him. It gave him time and space to think.

Lined with palm trees in the sparkling sun, the old buildings gave way to modern apartment blocks as they sped along. Unglamorous and regimented here on the outskirts of the city, they displayed more of the country's communist heritage.

It struck Mark how few adverts there were — none for petrol stations or burger outlets, none for fashions or hair products, or the multiple billboards there would have been back home.

There were just images of Fidel Castro and Che Guevara, glorifying the long-past revolution. These were interspersed with the odd café with lots of people mingling but very limited displays of food.

As they got on to the motorway proper, the scenery changed so that the modern apartment blocks faded away, and all there was to see was miles and miles of leafy lush vegetation.

With its tropical sun and regular rainfall, Mark thought this must be one of the greenest countries in the world. He knew that many people came to the more remote parts of the island because it was a haven for birdlife.

One good thing that had resulted from the lack of entrepreneurialism and development was that much of the island remained totally unspoiled, a veritable paradise for ecologists and nature lovers.

Lack of production meant lack of pollution and the preservation of wildlife habitats. In so many ways, Cuba was a small island stuck in a time warp.

As they reached a crossroads and had to stop, Mark turned to Bryony and saw she had drifted off to sleep. His heart went out to her and he felt a sinking feeling deep in his stomach. She looked very small curled up there with her scarf over her hair to keep it from tangling in the breeze from the open window.

Seeing it was slipping down, he carefully pulled it up again. For a second, he touched her hair. It was silky and gently waved.

Pippa's dead straight hair had been quite different. He hadn't thought of her much since this whole thing began.

Maybe a holiday was the best thing for him. Maybe he'd got too caught up in the maelstrom of his personal troubles and woes. He'd almost forgotten there was a great wide world beyond his personal one.

Perhaps his boss had been right and he needed to get completely out of his situation to see the wood from the trees, and reassess his life.

Even though he'd never wish difficulties on a good woman like Bryony, who had already experienced such tragedy, it felt good for him to have something new to worry about. He was pleased to be here for her.

He smiled wryly. Life was a series of worries, wasn't it, and a series of joys, ups and downs, sunshine and showers?

If he hadn't come here, he would never have met Bryony and he was beginning to like this stoical woman, a proud and caring mother who had spark and courage.

He put his hand back in his lap. Bryony needed his help badly and he just hoped this journey to Trinidad to find Anna was the right thing to do.

But who would know until they got there? Was it possible he was giving her hope where none existed?

Confidence was a good thing, it gave people something to follow, something positive to look to. He'd acted as if he was 100 percent confident in following this lead, simply because it was the only lead they had. They couldn't stay in Cuba for ever — they both had return flights booked and they would have to go back to real life soon.

He'd called the Cuban police this morning. He hadn't told Bryony, but they had virtually no leads at all and it was clear they were sceptical over whether Anna had been taken at all.

They came across a lot of young people who looked on Cuba's cheap rum and vibrant nightlife as a way to zone out and spend a few days non-stop partying. One lost teenager was no big deal to them.

Mark knew Bryony had spoken to the British Embassy but apart from making sympathetic noises, they had come up with nothing so far.

Mark knew he was Bryony's only hope. What's more, he believed her when she said Anna wasn't the partying kind. The girl sounded quiet, more focused on supporting her widowed mother and heavily into her art and studies. That wasn't the sort of girl to go on a drinking binge.

Mark had asked some of his police friends back home to do a bit of research, and look into Otto Weber for him. But that would take time, and getting any of their findings back to him in this country where communications weren't brilliant wouldn't be easy.

He watched the gentle rise and fall of Bryony's breathing and felt grateful that if nothing else, this journey would give her some rest. The dark shadows under her eyes had revealed that sleeping hadn't come easily to her lately.

A Dream to Share

The endless emerald fields continued to speed swiftly by them. It was clear that Norelvis was a good and careful driver, although Mark wished he wouldn't answer his mobile phone and gabble away in Spanish as he drove. The health and safety driving laws obviously weren't as firm in Cuba as they were in England and Mark had seen loads of people on their mobiles as they drove.

'That was my friend in Trinidad,' Norelvis said. 'He is Carlos, the father of an old schoolfriend. He runs a good place to stay, a *casa particular*, nice home on the edge of town, he speak English well. He is very good cook, makes good Cuban food. You eat dinner tonight, then we sleep. We go search for beautiful girl tomorrow, yes?'

'Yes. I hope he has maps and things

and can find the German man's house,' Mark said.

'Of course, we look at everything this evening. We have good meal, we make Mrs Bryony feel better, give her help to find Anna.'

'Yes, Norelvis, that would be good.'

'And my driving, that is good, too, good and safe, yes?'

'Yes, it's fine, you're doing well.' Mark could have done with a lad like him on the force back home, someone eager to please, optimistic and sensible. People took jobs and their relatively comfortable lifestyles for granted in England.

Here, they were going through a town and the houses were tiny. As they drove past, there were stray dogs in the street, skinny and abandoned. People were still smiley and welcoming but he saw a number of houses where a grandmother, mother and daughter with a young baby would wave as they went by. Three or even four generations living in one tiny house was not unusual.

'We have to cross the railway line here,' Norelvis said, 'but there is something up.'

They slowed down to a crawl. A number of policemen were guiding the long queue of noisy honking cars which also included horses and carts. People were transporting extraordinary loads, old motor bikes and washing machines, babies and elderly people and it was clear that for some, a horse and rickety old cart was their only form of transport.

As they had come to a halt, they could see a long line of people picking stuff up off the tracks. Mark sat up and peered. He simply couldn't make out what they were collecting so avidly. Norelvis got out, and conversed for a while in Spanish before he got back in. Bryony had woken but was still sleepy from her nap.

'What's happening?'

'It is just a Cuban thing,' Norelvis said. 'A train he has broken down and spilled his load, white sugar, on the tracks. As soon as people in the villages hear, they come out with anything they have — paper bags, bowls, brushes — anything to sweep up the sugar and take it home.'

'But you produce sugar cane here on the island, I've seen acres and acres of it. Why would they want to scrape it up from dirty train tracks?'

'True,' he shrugged his shoulders, 'but now the Russians are no longer friends of Cuba, we send all sugar to China and no-one has money here to turn it into lovely white sugar so they sell it back to us. But then it is too expensive for ordinary Cubans. So, when we have free sugar, even if it is on train tracks, everyone runs out to collect. It is precious, and they have little.'

'That's crazy,' Bryony said.

'Cuba is crazy. That's why we love it. We are living truly la vida loca.' Norelvis laughed and started up the car again and they drove off.

They passed through large towns,

tiny villages, and verdant farmland picturesque with snowy white egrets.

'Here we are, the beautiful little town of Trinidad,' he finally announced proudly.

At first viewing as they came down the hill, it hardly felt like a town at all, with just a few smallholdings here and there. Tomatoes ripened in the sun, chickens scrambled round, scraping their scrawny tasselled feet in the fertile earth.

The dirt road became wider and rows of houses, all the same, square, box-like with tiny walled front gardens and flat roofs appeared.

Townspeople carrying pineapples or guavas they had bought from stalls held hands with children, and grannies were ushered along beside them.

Then Bryony and Mark saw real live cowboys with stetsons, astride skinny horses. They nodded and smiled at the Oldsmobile as Norelvis carefully made his way slowly past so as not to upset the sleepy clopping horses.

Horse-drawn carts loaded with whole families or piled high with tangled spare parts of machinery trundled by, fast or slow depending on the age of their equine servants.

'Today is very important day,' Norelvis said, pointing to a truck. It was standing by one of the houses and hooked up to outside taps with hoses. 'This is the water truck. It delivers and everyone makes sure not to waste any drops.'

'You mean in a boiling hot country like this, you don't have piped water?'

'No. The water truck, we wait, sometimes it come, sometime not. But everyone very careful, they no waste no water, and collect rain until the truck come. Today is big celebration because the truck is here.'

As they trundled past in the Oldsmobile, they saw people sitting at the side of their houses where the truck had already been and a tiny trickle of water was making its way out of overflow pipes. The householders were holding jugs or large plastic containers, not wasting a single thimbleful.

'Gosh, that makes me feel bad about leaving the tap running at home when I clean my teeth,' Bryony said. 'Things are so different here, everything's in short supply except the sunshine.'

'And the smiles,' Norelvis said. 'We never fail to smile even if we have no water, no sugar, no big house. Because we have family. I have my brother, my mother and the most beautiful island on this beautiful earth. What more do I need?'

The Oldsmobile rocked and bumped over craters in the road. Mark had been trying to get a signal on his phone for ages without success. Now he had one pip up on his screen and as they approached the centre of town, a couple more appeared.

Then a bleep to say he had a message. It was Simon Brent, his police colleague.

Phone me as soon as poss.

Mark felt a surge of adrenaline. This

sounded like good news, as if Simon had something useful. If so, it would be the first useful thing since they had set off for Trinidad.

If Simon had found something out about Otto Weber which would give Mark some assurance that he hadn't dragged Bryony here on a wild goose chase it would make him feel a lot easier and a lot more hopeful that they would find Anna safe and sound.

He looked at his phone and the signal had disappeared again.

He muttered a curse.

'What's wrong?' Bryony asked.

'I just need to make a call back home, that's all.'

'The signal, she is better near the big hotel.'

'Where's that?'

'By the historical square. I take you there.' Norelvis turned the steering wheel to manoeuvre the stately car down a tiny side street, scattering a crowd of chickens.

Soon they had pulled up alongside

the Iberostar Grand Hotel, a beautiful old colonial style building painted peppermint green with wide wrought iron balconies.

'Let's go in, I'll treat us all to a drink to say thank you, Norelvis,' Mark said.

'Me, in a big hotel?' Norelvis was wide-eyed.

'Of course, you deserve it for being such an excellent driver and getting us here safe and sound.'

Mark ordered them all daiquiris and they were greeted by a member of staff with cold damp facecloths, perfect after such a hot dusty drive. They wiped their necks and throats and felt much refreshed.

Norelvis looked to be in his element, so proud to be in a hotel for once instead of hanging around outside touting for business.

Mark went off to make his phone call to Simon, leaving Bryony and Norelvis to cool off in the air-conditioned bar.

'One day,' the boy said, sipping his

drink, his blue eyes bright and optimistic, 'I dream of a Cuba where I can own a little house of my own. I would like to be in a small town like Trinidad, away from the mad rush of Havana, but near the sea. In my little house will be my beautiful wife and five beautiful children.'

'Five?' Bryony smiled as she downed the cool sweet liquid. 'That'll keep you busy.'

'It will keep my wife busy. The house and the children are her job and she will not want me to be under her feet. For I will be the great taxi man. I have been saving since I was tiny boy. I washed cars and mended taxi bikes enough to buy my own taxi bike.

'With the little bit of money I earn each week, I am building up to have my own business. I will have three Oldsmobiles of my own. One will be in peppermint green just like this hotel, one will be in bright pink like lipstick and ladies will want it to carry them round, and one will be in yellow, like sunshine to brighten up the lives of the old people. I will polish my cars every morning before I take tourist peoples like yourself for rides along the sea.

'And I will have staffs, two boys like me starting out. When my children grow, I will teach them to be taxi driver. We will be big family firm. Biggest in the little town of Trinidad. That is my dream.'

'It's a good dream,' Bryony said.

'What is your dream, Mrs Bryony?'

'Well, I'd have to think about that.' Bryony twirled the thin-stemmed glass in her fingers. 'Once I thought it was to own a big house, with a big garden and have an interesting job. But now maybe . . .'

She hesitated. When your life had been thrown upside down like a spilled pack of cards, and you had no idea what hand you were going to be dealt, you were wary of dreams. You didn't like to hope for anything, in case it never happened. Hopes and dreams were scary things.

'Maybe a husband,' Norelvis said. 'You pretty lady, you need husband. All lady needs good husband.'

Bryony managed a smile. She had not even contemplated another man in Warren's place. Yet she did feel lonely at times, on a bright day back home when she would have liked to go for a walk hand in hand with someone and talk about everything and nothing in particular.

At nights, when she woke from a nightmare, turned for some comfort and found only the cold empty space beside her. Yes, she felt lonely then.

But no, another husband would never be on the cards for her, Bryony had decided. It was a dream too far.

'My only dream is to find Anna,' she said and Norelvis nodded his head sagely.

'Of course, we must find Miss Anna. That is only dream you need.'

Shocking Revelations

Mark came back from phoning Simon. He was still trying to get his head around the news he had just been given. Policing could at times be the worst job in the world because you learned things that could devastate other people's lives. You learned things that could destroy and hurt people when that was absolutely the last thing you wanted.

He looked at Bryony. Inside he was breaking up into little pieces. Nevertheless, he was not going to forget his professionalism now. Many times he had had to retain a poker face and reveal nothing. This was one of those times, yet he wished it wasn't.

'Did you get through?' Bryony asked. Her kind, sensitive face was expectant, her eyes wide.

He must keep what he'd learned a

secret. Trying to find the right time to tell Bryony what he'd been told was going to be one of the most difficult tasks he'd ever faced.

'Er, no,' he said.

Was lying to protect someone OK? He sincerely hoped so as he saw her face drop.

'The signal wasn't brilliant. I'll try again later. I think I need another drink,' Mark said as a waiter came and took their orders.

It would give him time to get his head round what he'd learned. As he stood at the bar, his mind ticked over his conversation with Simon . . .

'Did you manage to dig anything up for me, Simon?'

'I did, finally. I don't have anything yet on your German guy, Otto Weber. I'm still trying. I've had a word with our friends in Interpol in Wiesbaden, they're working on that one for me. But while I was waiting, I thought I'd just take a look at Bryony Kemp and her family. You don't have too much to go on out there in Cuba, so I thought I'd just hunt around a bit, you know me, always keen on the detail.'

'Yup, that's why I asked you to look into this for me. Spit it out, Simon.'

'You're not going to like what you hear, Mark. Did you know Warren Kemp, Bryony Kemp's husband, was being investigated at the time of his death?'

This was certainly news to Mark and, he suspected, it would have been news to Bryony, too.

'No, what for?'

'Possible tax evasion, possible receiving of stolen goods. The guy was in trouble.'

'What sort of trouble? Why was he being looked into?'

'The guy had his fingers in loads of pies; small ones, nothing definite, nothing defined. It's just that he knew a few shady people and he seemed to have more money than an IT geek would normally.

'The trouble was, Kemp was a

gambler on the quiet. He travelled for work a bit and did the gambling stuff either on the internet, so his wife didn't learn about it, or far from home. He also liked to dabble in a little art trading and he was quite good at it. If he hadn't gambled the proceeds away, he could have made a good living at it.'

'Art trading?'

'Mmm. That was just one of his little sidelines. He'd been selling the odd picture here and there for years. Little pieces, things that go under the radar but net around five to ten grand. Seems he managed to hide it from everyone, his wife included.

'Thing is, no-one seems to know where the paintings came from. He wasn't stupid, he never sold in the same city twice and even then it was only the occasional sale, maybe one a year. He always came up with the same story, that it had been left him by an aunt, a German aunt.'

'Does he have a German aunt?'

'Not that we could find.'

'So where was he getting these paintings?'

'No idea. The investigation went cold. There was nothing that could be pinned on him. Then the guy upped and died and the team looking into him had other fish to fry. Warren Kemp is just a cold case now, sitting on the books doing nothing.'

'Did anyone think of the possibility they were forgeries? I worked on a case, many years ago, where a guy was fencing paintings. Turned out he had a friend who churned them out. Good forgeries they were — they could have kept up a nice little trade, only they got too greedy and were found out. It's just a thought.'

'Dunno, I don't think they got that far. It's a possibility, though, I suppose.'

'Thanks, Simon. You'll let me know if you come up with anything else, won't you? And Simon . . . '

'Yes?'

'Was there at any stage in the investigation any hint that Warren Kemp's wife

Bryony might be involved?'

'No.' Simon was definite. 'They looked into her, and the daughter. Both are as clean as a whistle. Innocent bystanders, you might say. I feel sorry for them.'

'Do they need to know?'

'Sometimes I think our jobs as policemen are to protect the innocent as well as prosecute the guilty. It's your call, of course, Mark, you're the one on the ground, so to speak. But personally I can't see much merit now in telling Bryony Kemp.

'I just told you because I thought you ought to know. What good would it do to tell a wife her dead husband was a bit of a gambler behind her back, and his habit was threatening to get out of control?'

Warren Kemp hadn't run up huge debts. He was keeping his head above water, like lots of gamblers do before it all goes pear-shaped. If the investigation had continued perhaps there would have been something to pin on him.

But there was nothing concrete at present, so what good would it do to give his wife more grief?

Mark had had to walk outside for a moment or two to gather himself before going back to face Bryony. Even now, standing at the bar, he felt unsettled.

What the devil had Warren Kemp been involved in? What other shady dealings might he have kept from his wife and his daughter?

Did anything he was up to when he was alive have a bearing on his daughter's sudden disappearance?

Bryony was fragile enough without learning something bad about the husband she hero-worshipped. She'd already had her world rocked by his death.

She had finally started to move on with her life. This trip was the last stage in her rehabilitation from widow to fully functioning woman.

It was bad enough her daughter had disappeared. She was doing her utmost to keep it together but what if Anna's disappearance or abduction or whatever had something to do with dodgy dealings her husband had been involved in and of which she had not even a notion?

Mark had been in policing long enough to recognise a hunch when he felt one coming on. He could feel a hunch in his blood that Warren Kemp's dodgy dealings perhaps had something to do with this whole sorry mess.

Kemp was the one who had been keen to come to Cuba. He was the one who had booked everything, had decided where the family was going to stay.

Did the holiday have something to do with the underhand lifestyle he'd so successfully hidden from his wife?

What's more, could Bryony possibly survive having her faith rocked that much? And if they did discover something really bad about Warren, how awful that she couldn't ask him, couldn't ask him questions.

The guy was dead, there would be so

much unanswered. How would she ever get over that?

The more he thought about it, the more Mark's head swam. As he went back with the drinks trying to hide his swirling thoughts, he was touched by how small she looked perched on her chair. And how kind she was being to Norelvis, patting his arm, praising him for the quality of his driving and bigging him up.

Here was a good woman who spent her life enhancing the world of those around her, caring for her daughter, trying to keep it together.

He downed his drink and watched them enjoy theirs. She might as well, for whatever revelations the future held, he was sure they wouldn't be easy ones to digest.

A Warm Welcome

'Now we go to see my friend Carlos and see his *casa particular*, yes?'

'You must be tired after that journey,' Mark said to Bryony.

She was touched by this man's care of her.

It was nice to be looked after for once. She'd spent so much time looking after Anna, and looking after Warren, it occurred to her, as they left the hotel and got back in the car.

Warren was the sort of guy who could spend hours at his computer. Working; he'd always seemed to be working. She'd take him up a cup of coffee in the evening and tell him he ought to get up and stretch a bit, but he'd always be poring over that keyboard.

He went away so often for work, and she knew it was hard for him staying in hotels, away from his family. Living out of a suitcase so often couldn't be much fun.

She'd always got his clothes ready and done his packing.

It was her way of saying 'I'm with you, even when we're in two different countries'.

Bryony had asked Warren on the odd occasion about his work, but he didn't like to talk about it.

'I spend enough time doing it.'

He would smile and close his laptop whenever she came to deliver another coffee.

'I don't want to talk about it endlessly, you're far more interesting. Tell me, how was work today?'

She had a part-time job at the local bookshop which she loved. She also loved telling Warren funny stories about the people who came in to buy books.

There was the couple, a husband and wife, who would order and come in to collect every new book about Elvis Presley.

It was surprising people were still

writing books about the legendary singer even though he was long gone.

Bryony found it difficult not to chuckle every time they came in. They both wore black leather Elvis jackets and tight Elvis trousers.

Both had jet black dyed hair. He wore his in the spitting image of his idol, but even his wife, though her hair was long and down to her waist, sported an Elvis quiff.

Every time Bryony regaled Warren with stories about them, she'd delight in his laughter. It was good to entertain a man who worked so hard, before he opened his laptop again to go back to whatever IT project it was he was toiling over.

Bryony would go off to read, but she was always aware she had to entertain her husband or he'd work himself into the ground.

She suspected that hard work was what had caused his heart attack.

It made her terribly sad that, try as hard as she could to make life easier for him, doing the washing, cleaning the house, entertaining him, she hadn't been able to stop him working himself to death.

Now, though, here was Mark, looking after her, bringing her drinks and making sure she was comfortable.

It occurred to her that Warren never really had done that.

He had been interesting, able to converse at length with Anna about her art history, and full of intellectual energy, but he wasn't one to do the simple things like bring her a cup of tea or cook her a meal.

She'd relied on her own work in the bookshop to give her relief from all the work at home. Even through the grief, she'd managed to go in every day she was scheduled.

It had helped to distract her from Warren's untimely death, and there was nothing better than burying her head in a book to try to forget.

★　★　★

They had arrived at the house of Norelvis's friend Carlos, who came out to greet them like long-lost friends.

'Welcome, welcome to Trinidad,' he said in excellent English. 'Here, let me help you with your bags.'

It was a very pleasant house, a cut above the others in the dusty street. Where the others had simple white-washed walls or plain grey concrete, Carlos's had Spanish patterned tiles.

Inside was a small but welcoming hallway with cool tiled floors and potted palms. A gate at the end of the passageway looked out on to a little garden with clucking chickens running about and, in the distance, the rolling Cuban hills.

'How long have you been running your guest house?' Bryony asked.

'About five years now. I am a teacher in the local college, as is my wife. She is off with my two children, staying with her mother on the other side of town.

'All our relatives are close by: aunts, uncles, in-laws, cousins all within walking distance. That's the way we like it in Cuba, the family is everything.'

There was a room for Bryony, and one for Mark.

Both were small but very cosy, with a table and chair for reading, a small TV and a balcony running across the back of the house.

It was common to both rooms and had ancient metalwork, cushioned chairs and a table for drinks.

'Now,' Carlos told them, 'I will show you the room where you will be having your meals.'

At the front of the house, the small dining-room looked over the road and again had French windows and a large wrought-iron balcony.

But it was such a quiet sleepy little road, with just children playing, horses and carts rolling by and the odd cowboy on horseback wandering back into the hills.

Bryony guessed it would be lovely to sit here over dinner or breakfast and watch the world drift by.

'Now.' Carlos looked proud as he stretched his arms, looking more like the lord of the manor than the owner of a small *casa particular*. 'This is where I shall later serve dinner. What food do you both like most?'

'Anything is fine,' Bryony said.

'Me, too, I'm not fussy.' Mark nodded.

'Good, I shall go off to the market now and buy provisions. Today, I hear they have had in excellent fish, if you like that and shellfish, I shall do you a typical Cuban fish stew. I am a good cook.'

'I can second that,' Norelvis said. 'I am only sorry I will not be staying to eat Carlos's food.'

'Are you not staying here with us?' Bryony asked.

'No, I have another friend a few roads away. I shall stay with him, and be available whenever you need taxi.

'Just call me on telephone. Carlos, he has the number.'

After the long drive, Bryony needed a

rest and a wash and brush up, so she and Mark agreed to meet for an early dinner at seven and parted.

An Alarming Plan

Carlos turned out to be an excellent cook, proud of his dish of steaming white fish chunks and prawns served in a delectable sauce of tomatoes, garlic, cumin, cilantro, capers and sofrito which was a Cuban speciality, a delicious onion sauce.

'I add just a tiny few flakes of chilli. It is big flavour, not big heat, which defines Cuban food. I hope you like it, and the accompaniment, *Moros y Cristianos*, traditional rice and black beans. Enjoy.'

It turned out to be the best meal Bryony had had since she arrived in Cuba. Full of zingy spice but not too hot.

As they ate, the net curtains at the French window billowed in the welcome breeze.

The sound of horses' hooves gently

clip-clopped below, mixed with the calls and greetings of one Cuban to another, enjoying the arrival of evening with its chance to relax after the labours of the day.

After the meal, Mark invited Carlos to drink coffee with them.

'We need to pick your brains, Carlos.'

Mark explained how Anna had gone missing.

Carlos's face was lined with concern.

'This is very bad. If someone has been a part of kidnapping your daughter, I will do everything I can to help. This is not the Cuban way: we are a law-abiding country. You are safer here than anywhere in the world.'

'Tomorrow,' Mark said, 'we need to find this house. We are going to ask Norelvis to drive us there, but it does look as if it is way up in the hills.

'Do you think the Oldsmobile will make it? The last thing we want is for him to get into trouble with his brother for pushing the car too much.'

Mark handed Carlos the piece of

paper with the address.

'Oh, no.' Carlos frowned as he read the address. 'You will not get an Oldsmobile up there. Not even a truck is good. This is miles up into the hills. An old sugar plantation, now a very grand residence but well off the beaten track.

'The only way to get to the Pedro Plantation is on horseback.'

'Horseback? Seriously?'

'Yes, it is about three hours' ride.'

'Three hours! But I've hardly ever been on a horse.' Bryony was aghast. 'And certainly not for hours on end.'

'But it is no problem.'

Carlos laughed at her dismay.

'We ride the horses all the time, they are quiet, calm beasts. The horses of Trinidad know the way. There are very few tracks through the hills and they just follow them until you tell them to stop.

'It is not difficult — easier than driving a car.'

Bryony wasn't in the least bit

convinced. Didn't horses bolt and rear up, throwing people off?

And didn't hours in the saddle make you ache until you felt you would never walk again?

Besides, she had only brought skirts with her. Surely she would need a pair of jodhpurs, or at least a pair of jeans? If she didn't have those, wouldn't she be chafed to the point of agony? After all, not only would it be three hours there, it would be three hours back, too!

The prospect of six hours non-stop in a hard leather saddle, not knowing how to do that bobbing up and down thing which people recommend, filled Bryony with horror.

Nevertheless, if they were going to find and save Anna, this seemed to be the only way.

'Do you know anyone who has horses we can hire?' Mark asked.

'Yes, I have a friend who owns a small farm; it is the first one at the end of this road, in the foothills. I can telephone when I go downstairs and see what he can do for us.'

'Does he have a guide who could go with us?'

Bryony was pleased that Mark was thinking this all through. The scariness of it was stopping her mind from functioning properly.

'You could not have a better guide than Norelvis. He used to spend many school holidays here. The boy has been up in those hills countless times to go swimming in the cool mountain streams in the height of summer. That boy loves horses almost as much as he loves cars.'

'Then that's a done deal,' Mark said.

He looked over at Bryony and for the first time, touched her, putting a gentle hand on her arm.

'Do you have any rum, Carlos? I think Bryony could do with a little bit of Dutch courage to get her used to the idea.'

Carlos chortled.

'You ask a Cuban if he has rum? I have the finest.'

Carlos went over to a polished

sideboard in the corner and poured them all a large shot.

'Cheers,' he said as he raised his glass. 'To adventure, my friends, and to finding your Anna.'

Bryony finished her glass in one, realising that her heart had been beating twenty to the dozen at the news they were going pony trekking in a strange country without any warning.

As soon as the fiery liquid hit her bloodstream, she could feel its calming effect.

She decided to forget her troubles for the time being and try to enjoy the evening for what it was, a chance to relax before their big journey tomorrow.

When Mark suggested that they go for an evening walk around Trinidad, she decided that would be a lot better than sitting worrying about Anna and about tomorrow's journey.

It Takes Two

Bryony and Mark took a right turn out of Carlos's house and wandered down the road. Trinidad was both a sleepy place and a lively one. People sat on steps taking in the night air as the sky darkened and the stars appeared.

Caribbean spices and woodsmoke drifted on the breeze as people cooked their supper. Cobbled streets with gaily coloured yellow and turquoise houses led to the main square ringing with the bells of taxi bikes.

From a bar near the square, salsa music rang out.

'Fancy a drink?' Mark asked.

'I'm not sure I should have another one,' Bryony confessed. 'I feel a little woozy.'

'You are still on holiday, you know, and it'll help to calm you. I'm not saying you should forget about Anna but you can't think of her every single moment, or it'll drive you mad. Remember, I promised you, we will find her.'

With this reassurance ringing in her ears, Bryony sat at one of the chairs near the open square.

'What would you like?'

'Surprise me.'

She sat and watched the Trinidad nightlife.

Lovers wandered by, hand in hand, mothers and fathers with babes in arms, middle-aged couples sat and chatted with friends at tables, and elderly people escorted by their teenage grandchildren wandered to and fro.

It was a marvellous mêlée of old and young, all enjoying and celebrating the joys of a beautiful night and the uplifting beat of the music.

Mark came back with two creamy pina coladas with their cooling crushed ice and foamy tops.

'You look lovely this evening,' he said. The compliment surprised her.

She'd worn nothing special, just a white dress with lace at the neck and hem, her hair scraped back, no make-up, her limbs tanned.

'I think all you're seeing is healthiness.' She blushed. 'It must be all the fresh fruit and sunshine.'

As they talked, the musicians inside the bar came out on to the pavement, carrying their instruments and playing a slow salsa number. The vocalist crooned about *mi corazon*, my heart, one of the few Spanish words Bryony understood.

But she was sure it wasn't a breaking heart as the tune was too sweet for that.

Perhaps he was singing about new love when it first blossoms.

A mixed group of people spontaneously got up to dance. A lady in her eighties had been gently taken by the hand by an elderly man in a wheat-coloured linen suit, with a fedora at a jaunty angle.

The two of them entwined, half holding each other up, but moving together in perfect time, like reeds blowing in the breeze.

A girl and boy of around ten took each other's hands apparently without thinking and soon there were half a dozen people of all ages making the most of the Caribbean evening.

Mark held out his hand.

'Do you dance?' he asked.

'Oh, hardly at all.'

Bryony hesitated, yet the rhythms were so captivating, the beat so elemental, she desperately wanted to move to the music, to feel it free her from her troubles.

She remembered the classes she and Warren had gone to a couple of years ago. They had both enjoyed them, until he had lost interest.

He kept promising to come, but in the end he always found he couldn't make it. He was busy, he said, with work on his computer. She'd had to persuade a girl friend to go instead to the next class.

The steps had become ingrained in

her memory. As Bryony watched the people's feet now, she remembered the familiar patterns.

'I'm sure you could manage this one. Come on, it's not a fast one, it'll be easy.'

Mark got up and suddenly, almost as if she had been given a magic charm, her feet were bewitched into following his.

His hands entwined around hers, leading her expertly in front of him and behind him, into a slow twirl, out of a gentle hold.

She felt the hem of her skirts brush her knees, and the tip of her nose brushed by her own ponytail as he turned her round and round, in and out of the intricate designs their bodies were making.

The town square of Trinidad, the stars above, the street below her feet, all swam before her as her body moved of its own accord, as if Mark was twirling her on a string.

He was careful to guide and lead her

so that the two of them were perfectly in time with the rise and fall of the drum beat, the lilting guitars, the soft shake of maracas.

In no time at all it was as if she was in a dream, as if time was standing still, as if she had floated up in a gentle maelstrom and was whirling and turning, her feet not even connected to the ground.

She would have been happy to dance like that for ever, feeling the musical notes, and the warmth of Mark's hands brushing hers, and the sensation of the strong muscles in his back as she held him and he held her.

It was as if the musicians were playing only for them, as if there were no other dancers there and they were in their own private trance.

Sadly, very sadly, the music came to an end.

Bryony was in such a daze, she was grateful to Mark for leading her smoothly back to her seat and easing her into her place at the table. She was experiencing the same light-as-air feeling as after a massage at the beauty parlour.

It was as if she had taken a calming drug and for those few moments she hadn't thought about anything other than being in the moment.

It was such a release, such a joy, and as Mark sat down and smiled at her, something occurred to her. This was the first time she had felt relaxed and totally comfortable with another man since she had lost Warren.

Why, she wondered, had Warren stopped finding the time to come dancing with her?

She knew work seemed to take up all his time, but she'd never asked him to work that hard. She had never been one of those wives who pushed their husbands to make more and more money, either. In fact, she had asked him on a number of occasions to slow down.

What's more, he had found time to go out with his mates. Yet she had been forced to go dancing with her girl friend.

He always maintained he was too busy yet it would only have been a couple of hours and she would have enjoyed it so much.

It was an uncomfortable feeling that ripped through her mind, almost like being disloyal to him. That was a terrible thing to do when someone had died.

Yet she had been loyal to him when he was alive in so many, many ways.

It would have been so nice if they could have shared together once more the sort of experience she had just shared with Mark. Had she ever really known her husband, she wondered.

How well could you really know anyone, even the man you were married to?

'Maybe we should go back now. We've got a busy day ahead, and I don't want to tire you out,' Mark said.

'Yes, thank you for that, I needed it. You lead well.'

'You follow well. After all, it takes two.'

That was true, Bryony thought, it takes two.

They walked past the multi-coloured houses, their turquoises and sunshine yellows, their oranges and berry pinks lit up by bulbs strung along them like fairy lights.

She was suddenly acutely aware of Mark walking beside her, of the warmth of his body next to her, of the tiny touch of the blond hairs on his arm tickling her bare skin.

It takes two, he'd said.

And for the first time ever, she admitted that perhaps hers and Warren's marriage wasn't as totally and utterly in tune as she'd always liked to think.

Or more to the point, persuaded herself it was.

It takes two . . .

Those words rang in her ears until she finally laid her head on the pillow and fell into a fitful sleep.

So Near and Yet So Far

The next morning, Bryony heard voices in the dining room and quickly got washed and dressed. When she went down, Mark and Carlos were in earnest conversation over a steaming coffee. Bowls of fruit salad, yoghurt and freshly baked rolls with butter and jam were laid out.

'You have a superb country here,' Mark was saying. 'It was really lovely last night to see all the generations enjoying themselves together. There's a lot we could learn from that back home in the UK.'

'Yes, our land is superb,' Carlos nodded his head, 'but sadly still a little behind the times. It pains me when I watch the rest of the world surging forward and leaving us behind.

'You see over the road there? You cannot have failed to notice that my neighbour keeps a lovely big fat pig in his front garden!

'We have to use every scrap of land we have. I grow much of my own food, my own tomatoes and salads. We have to live a semi-rural life even in this busy little tourist town.

'It is not because we have a hankering for the old country ways. It is because supplies of everything are so fitful.'

'I noticed,' Bryony said as she sat down and buttered a roll, 'that you use these tiny packets of butter, but they come from Europe. I noticed the same thing in the hotel.

'Why would you ship them half the way across the world when you have this lush green countryside which would be perfect for cows?'

Carlos nodded.

'Ah, yes, that is sad, is it not? We do not produce many of our own goods but have to import things we could easily grow and make here. The trouble is, we have no entrepreneurs.

'This is because the ordinary people have not much money to spend and there is almost zero competition. With no-one apart from the tourists to buy goods, nobody bothers to make them. We are all living the life we might have lived one hundred years ago.'

He shrugged.

'Take soap. You cannot get good soap for love nor money. Yet it is not a difficult thing to make. We just do not have your Body Shop or your Jo Malone or any of these amazing brands I see all over the internet. I have tried them. Sometimes, when guests stay who have been to Cuba before and know how few things there are here of high quality, they will leave things they no longer need.

'Then I think, why do we not produce such lovely things? Yet who would buy it? We are locked into a system which keeps us a backward country, even though we can see the shores of America and the rest of the world on a clear day.'

He shrugged.

'One day it will all change. One day soon. I already see it changing now. My children will live in a very different Cuba when they are my age.'

'The big question will be,' Mark replied, 'whether with that newfound prosperity, you will lose some of the tight bonds of family and whether grandchildren will dance together in the streets with their grandparents. It would be a shame to see that go.'

As they sat in thought and finished off their breakfast by the open window, there was the sound of hooves and then a shout from below.

Carlos got up to look over the balcony. There followed an animated conversation in Spanish.

'My friend has arrived with your horses, and Norelvis has come to accompany you into the hills. Let me go and get them some coffee and fill the water bottles for you while you finish your breakfast. Then you can be off.'

★　★　★

Mark could see Bryony had concerns about the journey ahead. At this moment, she was peering out with a worried expression, watching the horses snorting and scuffing their hooves in the dirt.

He went and stood next to her to reassure her. As he did so, he noticed her curls lifting in the breeze. Last night, as they had danced, he had desperately wanted to stroke those curls, to feel their softness running through his fingers, to tell her everything would be OK.

He had seen people involved in investigations like this — disappeared children, absent brothers and sisters. He wanted to tell her that often people just desired to go off on their own. The idea of running away was a very attractive one.

Who hadn't thought about doing that when they were a child?

Might Anna just have become worn

down with all her obligations, perhaps what she saw as the responsibility of looking after a distraught mother?

Mark couldn't possibly say that to Bryony, though; it would destroy her. He knew as a policeman that many people with fewer problems than Anna had been attracted to taking off somewhere where no-one knew them.

The draw of disappearing, even for a short time, could be strong enough to take people away from a loving family. Often people had done exactly that, then they were found and all was well.

But this was different. The thought had crossed his mind, and he was sure it must also have crossed Bryony's, that Anna had willingly gone off with someone.

Had she found coping with her grief, and her mother's grief too difficult?

She was very young to have such a burden to carry. If someone had offered her some kind of respite might she not take it — an older man, perhaps offering a trip to somewhere a bit more exotic than her mother would contemplate, the chance to see some real Cuban life?

The chance to have her first experience as an adult might have appealed to a girl who felt trapped.

Dark shadows underneath Bryony's eyes betrayed a night spent tossing and turning and the way she kept checking and rechecking her rucksack made him want to reassure her.

He went over to where she was gazing down at the horses, and took a look over the balcony.

'Goodness,' he said in surprise, 'they're little more than ponies. They'll be no trouble at all to ride.'

'Do you think so?'

'I'm used to the great big beasts they use as police horses. I once thought of going into the mounted police but then I chose a different route. Being a detective always seemed more interesting. Police horses are huge great things. We'll have no trouble on those two, they'll be as tame as donkeys.'

He saw her shoulders, which had been hunched, relax a little.

He took a chance, a big chance, and rested his hand on her arm

Ever since last night, when she had melted into his touch, willingly responding to his lead when they were dancing, he'd imagined what it would be like to feel the warmth of her skin again. But concerns about whether she might flinch away from his touch, about whether she still held a candle burning bright for her husband had run round in his head.

She didn't pull away. In fact, she seemed to melt slightly. He saw her breathing slow down.

'It'll be fine,' he reassured her. 'Just think, Bryony, you might enjoy it. It might even be fun.'

She looked up at him and her eyes were big and soulful, but he was delighted to see the corners of her mouth upturn slightly in the ghost of a smile.

All of a sudden, from nowhere, the

thing he most wanted to do in all the world, was take her in his arms and kiss her.

He knew it would be unwise but sometimes it was easy to be carried on an emotion if it was strong, like a force of nature. But she looked so vulnerable, so gorgeous standing there in her white cotton shirt, devoid of make-up, looking up at him, appealing for his help to get her through this ordeal.

He placed another hand on her and turned her to him. For a moment, for one searing, extraordinary, uplifting moment, she turned her face up to his, and he saw her eyes flicker.

He leaned down, a fraction closer. So close he could smell melon and mandarin shampoo on her hair, detect jasmine from the soap she had used.

She had moved one tiny fraction closer to him and her lips had parted. Any second now, their lips would touch. He realised he wanted that more than anything.

His heart beat faster, his breath

became shallow, adrenaline coursed through his veins at the nearness of her.

It wasn't like last night. Last night was in full view of other people, last night he had been in control and she had followed. This fresh, bright morning, they were like a male and female deer who had come across each other in a forest clearing, were edging around each other, tilting heads to get to know each other, a beam of sun settling upon them like a blessing.

Any false move and he sensed she would back away.

Mark knew he wanted to kiss Bryony. What's more, he knew she wanted to kiss him. This was his chance to show her how he felt.

He moved closer, deciding to be brave, to take the moment and make it theirs. Then, suddenly, the door burst open.

Carlos didn't see them. Mark moved back like a shot, knowing Bryony would be embarrassed.

The moment was lost. Mark had

been too hesitant, his timing was wrong. He could have kicked himself for being a stupid, hesitant, fool. Would that moment ever come again?

No Turning Back

'The horses are ready, come down and try them.' Carlos ushered them out and on to the street.

'They look awfully big,' Bryony said nervously.

'Yours is smallest. Here, let me help you.' Norelvis guided her foot into the stirrup. 'Now, just put your hands, one here on pommel, one here on back of saddle. Put your foot on my hands, use it as stirrup, then up.'

In a second she was sitting astride the animal. He shook his mane but seemed unconcerned to have such a light weight on his back.

Would he be able to tell how inexperienced she was? Would he play up, or, heaven forbid, decide at some point he wanted to gallop, and shake her off?

'Yours is called Bembe,' Norelvis said

as he adjusted the stirrups and tightened the girth.

He beckoned to Mark to mount.

'Your one, he is called Tolomeo. Bembe is very lazy and likes to eat whenever he sees a tasty leaf, so I go at back to make him keep going. If he stop, Mrs Bryony, just give him little prod with your heels in side, like this.'

Norelvis had mounted himself by now, his horse somewhat larger and sturdier then theirs, which were tough, wiry stock.

'Tolomeo knows the way even if we go to blindfold him. He is leader of men, just like you, Mr Mark. He has job to do and he does it. He will take us into hills to find Miss Anna.'

'They're different from English horses somehow,' Bryony commented to Mark as Carlos waved them goodbye.

They clip-clopped off up the road which soon turned into a dirt track leading out of Trinidad.

'These horses are bred for work

rather than play. No-one spends hours grooming them.'

Mark patted Tolomeo and a little cloud of dust came out of his coat as if to prove a point.

'But they are lovely in their ragged, homely, Cuban way.'

Bryony had to agree as she stroked Bembe and he tossed his head in his bright orange rope bridle.

'Here is outskirts of village,' Norelvis announced as they came to a gate.

He expertly removed the rope around it and ushered them through.

'Now we climb.'

And climb they did, through verdant fields, up rock-strewn pathways, past acres of sturdy tobacco with their leaves like green men's hankies hung out to dry in the hot air.

They continued through the high stems of sugar cane sprouting their sweet delectable shoots like sherbert fountains.

The obedient horses trotted nobly along. All the while, Norelvis delighted in his new role as horse-trekking tourist guide.

He told them who owned this little farm, how he had been chased by a dog at that smallholding.

Laughing heartily, how he had been sweet on the girl who lived up that winding track but that she was now very fat and besides, had a muscle-bound husband and three equally plump rosy-cheeked children.

Occasionally, carefully monitoring how they were doing, Norelvis would go to the front of their little party, and encourage the horses along faster.

In some unspoken pact, the two men worked together to make Bryony feel safe. Mark allowed his horse to slow and end up behind Bryony so that she was always sandwiched between them, in case her horse lost his footing on the rocks and stones.

Bryony soon was confident enough to try trotting and although it was terrifying, it was also exhilarating. Holding on for dear life, her knees clamped around the horse's flank, her hand gripping the pommel, it felt good to be going fast.

She'd even managed, by watching Norelvis's natural technique, to acquire the bouncing motion which made her feel finally in control of her steed.

Who would have thought, she couldn't help musing, that she would be out in the wilds of Cuba, without Warren to lean on, riding a horse for hours on end? And that she'd actually be enjoying the sensation, the freedom of being in control of her own destiny?

It occurred to her that she had come to rely on Warren perhaps too much. He was such a strong character, quite dominating, in fact.

Had she fallen into a mode whereby she let him take all the important decisions, and she took a back seat to him, she wondered.

She'd almost come to believe that she wasn't good at doing things, that she always had to defer to him. Yet here she was, coping perfectly well in a trying and difficult situation.

Anna was missing, yet she'd gone out to find her. Bryony knew she'd suffered crippling anxiety following Warren's death. No wonder, when she relied on him so much.

All that searching for stuff endlessly in her handbag during the journey out here, all that feeling she couldn't cope, all the times she had wanted to rush back home where the four walls would protect her, the way her heart had pounded as if her chest was about to explode . . .

Even last night, lying awake, worrying about how much being on a horse for hours would hurt, whether her back and legs could stand it.

Now, here she was, not just coping, but actually enjoying the ride!

She could do things, she could be independent, she could take a stand. On her own.

Had Warren slowly, subtly, during their marriage actually undermined her without her even noticing? Had he played on his expertise on the computer and his wide knowledge of the world and all its ways to make her feel incapable, to try to control her somewhat?

She'd certainly spent a lot of her life running round after him, catering to his every whim, making sure he was happy, well fed and watered whilst he spent hours working away and . . . ignoring her.

Sometimes her friends had ticked her off, saying she was like a servant in his company, just waiting for him to tell her what he needed, and putting his needs before her own.

That was one of the reasons, she realised, why she'd felt so devastated when he'd died — the thought that she couldn't do things on her own.

As she trotted along, a wide stretch of glorious emerald grass opened before them and Mark drew his horse to trot along by her side.

'How's it going?'

'Not bad — pretty good, actually.'

It was his steady, stalwart encouragement that had helped her get this far.

Without it, she might still be back in Havana, nervous and ruled by her anxiety, waiting in vain for the Cuban police to do something.

Mark hadn't pushed or controlled her into anything. He'd merely been there, by her side, a sensible authoritative voice, supporting her.

What's more, she hadn't once seen him bury himself in a phone or a computer.

He was a doer in the old-fashioned sense. Practical and straightforward, he interacted with the real world, not the virtual computer world.

It was refreshing; it had shown her what perhaps she'd been missing.

For once, her mind flitted to Warren and Bryony did not feel totally bereft by his passing.

Yes, it was sad, it was terrible for someone to die so young. It was devastating to lose her husband, the person she had pledged her life to.

But it had happened, and time had passed.

The world was full of people in her situation, and they had to get by. Life went on.

There was a future after you lost someone. There had to be, because there were new people who could care for you, without curtailing you, without holding you back. Without needing you to bow to their needs.

And there were others still alive you had to care for.

You had to be strong for them.

Searching for Clues

Mark was looking far into the hills as he rode next to her.

'I was just thinking about Anna,' Bryony said to him. 'Do you think we will find her at this plantation house, Mark? After all, what real evidence do we have that she is there?'

He gave her a serious look.

'You're having those sort of doubts that always enter one's mind at this stage in an investigation. You clutch at straws, at anything that will lead you one tiny, stuttering step forwards.

'Then, on your way to check it out, it's so often that you are beset by fears that it'll be a wild goose chase.'

He shrugged.

'Sometimes it is, but then there are crucial times it isn't. It's like trying to do a jigsaw without a picture to follow. You just have to keep trying to pick up various pieces, small and seemingly insignificant leads and clues, and put them together until you get the final picture.'

'I fear maybe we're too late.' Bryony was on the verge of tears.

'Look, if someone's taken Anna, they've taken her for a purpose. Whether she's been taken hostage for some reason or another, we set off as quickly as we could.

'There is no fast way to travel in Cuba. If she is being held at the country house, we're not going to be there long after her. If she's here, we'll find her. Don't give up hope. Instead, let's just go over the things we know.'

'That sounds like a plan,' Bryony said.

It would help to make the journey slide by more easily. They'd been going for two hours now without stopping.

She searched her memory, like a filing cabinet, for the things they had discovered so far.

'OK, first of all, there was the man

with the beard and the pot belly. I saw him around the hotel on a number of occasions, and you saw him, too, at reception on the day we arrived.'

'That's right, and the more I think about it, the more I'm sure he was taking photos of you, but more of Anna.'

'It might just be a coincidence,' Bryony said, 'but at the time he was taking those photos, she was chatting in German to a young guy in the queue.'

'And we know, from going to the cigar museum, that the bearded man taking the photos, Otto Weber, is German. Do you think he and the German lad in the queue were together?'

'No, definitely not,' Bryony said. 'The young guy was with a group of boys his own age. They were obviously students, probably on a gap year or on holiday from uni.'

'What I've been wondering,' Mark said, 'is what made Otto Weber so interested in Anna. Clearly she's very attractive and there could have been a motive there — he might have developed some sort of obsession with her. But I don't think that was it at all. Clearly, though, something about her sparked his interest.'

Bryony could feel her mind ticking over. She'd thought about things so much in the dark, quiet hours of night, but sparking ideas off someone else was much more fruitful.

'Do you think, perhaps, it might have been something to do with the fact that he heard her speaking in German to the lad in the queue?'

'Quite possibly. It's definitely a point linking Otto Weber and Anna together. I can't imagine there are many people in Cuba who speak German. How good is she at the language?'

'Very good,' Bryony said, 'almost fluent, in fact. She had a German penpal, Gisela, from a very early age. They're a lovely family and every year, Anna spends two weeks at Easter at Gisela's and Gisela comes to us for two weeks in the summer.'

She smiled.

'I used to joke with Warren that those two girls had secrets we would never know because neither he nor I speak a word of the language yet they used to natter endlessly in German. When they weren't together, they'd be writing letters, and they often phoned one another. Gisela's due to come and see us soon for her summer visit. German was one of Anna's A-levels and she flew through the exams with top marks. She even reads novels in German just for fun.'

'That could explain possibly why Otto Weber was following Anna — that she speaks near-perfect German, and he needed a German speaker for some reason.'

'Do you think he was following her, then? That's pretty creepy. And why would he be taking photos of her?' Bryony frowned.

'I do think he was following her, and I don't think it's a coincidence you saw him so much around the hotel. He was definitely tracking your movements.

'I hate to say it, but I don't think her disappearance was some sort of chance meeting. For some reason, it looks like Otto Weber plotted her abduction or, at the very least, tricked Anna into going with him.

'She was interested in art,' Mark continued, 'and he obviously knows a lot about it. It wouldn't have been difficult for him to lure her off, maybe with some promise of seeing interesting artworks, or meeting someone who might further her future career. Was she hoping for a career in the art world?'

'Yes, she was. In fact, she was desperate to do that for a living. She said to me on more than one occasion that her idea of torture would be to spend the rest of her life in an office. She was keen on working in a gallery or an auction room but as we don't know anybody in that field she realised it would be an uphill struggle.'

'So, we know that Otto Weber was

interested in Anna's looks, otherwise why would he take photos of her? We also know that he was interested in her ability to speak German. And that he's an art dealer and that he's wealthy, with that big house in Havana and the one here tucked away in the hills.'

'What else? There must be something that made him target her?'

Mark thought long and hard.

'Darn it, we missed a trick by rushing off like this on the first lead we were given to Anna's whereabouts. I should have done more research into Otto Weber's background.

'What we do know is that his servant is frightened of him, or frightened of something. She certainly didn't seem very open when we called at the Havana house. I thought she was very cowed, and anxious to get rid of us.'

'That's true. It certainly indicates he's into something dodgy.'

What they also knew, Mark thought, though he couldn't share it with Bryony just at that moment as she had too much else to deal with, was that Bryony's husband Warren was mixed up in some way with trading in art, quite possibly stolen.

What was it Mark's police contact back home had said he'd discovered? That Warren Kemp was dealing in art in a small way to fund his gambling habit.

That he had been acquiring paintings from somewhere and had been selling them on the quiet.

In Grave Danger

As they rounded a bend, Norelvis stopped them, and unusually for him, he looked serious.

'That is Otto Weber's plantation house.'

There in the distance, in the lee of a hill stood a mansion with wide verandahs. Once grand, it had a neglected air. Paint which had once been peppermint coloured now looked sad and faded.

One of the shutters had come from its moorings and hung on a slant. Columns at the front supporting a balcony above were chipped and needed painting. Around the house palm trees stood like tall green ostrich feathers, their plumes waving gently in the breeze.

'At one time,' Mark said, 'that would have been a magnificent house. It looks, though, like Otto Weber needs an injection of cash to keep such a fine place in order. It can't be easy financing this house as well as the one in Havana.

'I wonder if that's a clue as to why he's taken Anna.'

'But we don't have any money.' Bryony sounded bewildered. 'He can't have imagined that kidnapping Anna would result in a huge ransom. I'd gladly mortgage everything I've got to get her back, but it wouldn't amount to much.'

'We will tie up horses here.'

Norelvis jumped off and tethered the two horses to a tree, well hidden by tall bushes.

'It is best we approach house on foot, and from side. Here will be less likely for us to be seen.'

'Wait,' Mark said. 'It would be madness to go in daylight. We need the cover of darkness. Besides, we're hot and tired and hungry. It's been a long day. Let's just hunker down here where we can see the house but stay hidden.

'We'll take it in turns to keep watch while the others take a nap. That way, we can keep an eye on the place and try to suss out who might be around before we go creeping around there unannounced.

'But before that, let's have something to eat.'

From a leather bag slung round his shoulders which Carlos had given him, he took out some picadillo-filled empanadas.

Norelvis took a blanket from his saddlebags and laid out the food.

'I have home-made lemonade, cassava doughnuts and oranges.'

'It's a feast!' Bryony exclaimed. 'Thank you guys so much. I was too nervous this morning to think about bringing food and drink.'

'When you have been in these hills from a child, you remember always to bring sweet things and water to keep up energy. If not, you can always cut down sugar cane to eat. It is good, sweet and chewy. But you have to have machete.'

At this point, Norelvis whipped out a long bladed knife.

Mark urged him to put it back, realising Norelvis could be a bit too hasty and Latin in his hotheaded approach.

'We definitely won't be needing that,' Mark told him.

It was a feast, and Mark felt much revived after it. He could tell Bryony was beginning to flag, but was delighted to see her take her fill of the spicy mince and pepper pasties.

'You two get comfortable and take a nap first. I'll keep lookout. I've bought some binoculars.

'So far, all I can see is some horses in the paddock in front of the house and an old man bringing out feed. There's little else happening. Get some rest.'

'Are you sure?' Bryony asked.

'I can stay awake with you,' Norelvis offered.

'No, you get some sleep, you'll be more alert that way when we break in.'

'Break in?' Bryony looked alarmed.

'Yup, we've got to if we're going to rescue Anna.'

'But shouldn't we call the police?' Bryony asked.

'The police? Hah, do not bother with those in Havana,' Norelvis scoffed. 'They will do nothing. With a fine big house in Havana and a business making money, the police in my city will be very slow to do anything to upset the Big Man Otto Weber. He will have friends in high-up places.

'You would be better to bring in the Trinidad police, if any. This man is keeping his head, how you say, under the radar here, in this little town. He is hiding from everybody, the police included. He do not want them to know what bad business he does.'

'I think he's right, Bryony, let's just do this our own way for the time being. We're not even sure Anna's in there. If she is, we'll get her out. If not, at least we might find out some clues to where she is.'

Bryony and Norelvis settled down on the rugs and in a very short while, they were both fast asleep. Now, Mark thought, he could properly get to work.

This bit he needed to do on his own, so as not to endanger the others.

With great care not to disturb them, he crept away into the darkness. In the dark was the time to move towards the house, to discover its secrets.

Making his way with all the stealth of a panther, he stepped among the undergrowth. Dressed all in black, he faded well into the jungle undergrowth.

Outside, the house was quiet but inside, he could hear voices. Pressing himself to the wall at the front of the house, he edged his way along. The voices, gabbling in Spanish were coming from the kitchen.

He peeked through the window, and there was a cook dishing up steaming bowls of soup, and a maid placing them on a tray.

At the table in front of them was a beefy Cuban, tall and with hefty muscles, ripping open a loaf.

Without ceremony, he helped himself to one of the bowls of soup on the tray and was immediately told off by the cook. Obviously, she expected him to wait for his, when he had no intention of doing so.

He stuffed food into his mouth, waving their criticisms away. Mark saw a pistol strapped to his hip, and on the chair next to him a sizeable firearm. Otto Weber's guard was not a man to be messed with.

Backing away from the kitchen, Mark noted a pool of light to the front of the house. Bending down so as not to be seen from any windows, he made his way around.

When he got to the front, he could hear voices speaking alternately in German, Spanish and, more importantly, in English. His ears really pricked up when he heard a young girl's voice. Holding his breath, he strained to hear.

'It's not fair to lead her on like this. I won't do it any longer. I can't!'

'Yes, you can, and what's more you will. Don't you dare let that miserable look come on your face again. Keep smiling. Make out like we are having a chat about the jolly days back in Germany. Any moment now, she's going to take you into her confidence, I can tell. She likes you. You have played your part well.

'As soon as I get what I want, you can go. But not before. Remember that. Until I get what I want, you stay here.'

There was a pause.

'That's better, you are so much more pretty when you smile, dear Anna. Now, I can hear her coming back down the stairs. Laugh, like we are sharing a joke together.'

Mark heard a small laugh, but it was strained. What the devil was going on? Anna laughed again, then he heard her speak.

'I hate you! No wonder she never

trusted you, you filthy pig.'

Otto Weber let out a huge belly laugh, then abruptly stopped.

'Hello, Aunt. Come on, the soup is just about to be served.'

Mark, crouching on the ground, didn't understand the rest of the conversation which took place between Anna and what sounded like an old lady.

That must be the old woman he'd seen Otto Weber accompanying in Havana. She had looked very frail.

He heard the soup being brought in, then the mains and after a while, a dessert.

'She's tired now, darn it,' Mark finally heard Otto Weber say. 'She's fallen asleep in her chair. We won't get anything more out of her tonight.'

There was gentle snoring as the old lady dozed.

'I'm tired, too.' Anna had come over to the window for air and Mark could hear better now, even though she spoke softly. 'I'm tired of all this. It's wrong, so wrong.'

'Rubbish.' Otto Weber came to join her. 'You're young and idealistic. You'll learn when you reach my age that you have to take what's yours, by whatever means you can. She has stood in my way all my life. But you, you are my golden key.'

'I'm nothing of the sort and you'll regret what you've done once you're found out.'

'No-one will find out. I'll be long gone once I get what I want.'

'Please!' Anna was pleading now, and it made Mark's blood boil to hear it. 'Just let me get back to my mother. She'll be desperately worried about me, it's cruel to let her suffer like that.'

'What do I care about your foolish mother? If she had more sense, she wouldn't be in the position she's in now. Listen to me.' Mark heard him hiss through gritted teeth. 'You'll do my bidding or you'll disappear from your poor dear mother's life for ever.

'There are lots of deep mountain pools in these hills. You don't want to end up with a boulder tied to your ankles at the bottom of one of them, do you? I could get Manuel to snuff you out like a candle between his finger and thumb, so you'd never see your mother again.

'Get up, I've had enough of you. Manuel will escort you to your room.'

'Escort me? March me like a prisoner you mean.'

Anna sniffed, close to tears, but her spirit clearly wasn't broken.

Mark heard Weber get up, open the door and yell at the top of his voice. The sound of clumping boots and a grunt heralded the arrival of Manuel and Mark heard their footsteps die away.

The sudden filling of the air with cigar smoke told Mark that Otto Weber had decided to sit with the old lady and smoke while he worked out his next move.

Mark knew he must find out where Anna's bedroom was. Slowly, carefully, he stretched his limbs, which had stiffened up through standing still for so long.

He moved from the front of the house round to the side, peering up at the rooms in the house, desperate to see a light which would indicate which room Anna was being taken to.

All the rooms on the ground floor had wrought-iron bars at the windows for security. Mark hoped she wasn't being taken upstairs.

Bingo! He saw a ground floor light come on at the back of the house. Very carefully he made his way to it.

The windows were open to try to make the most of the little night breeze there was on the air.

From the darkness, Mark saw Anna enter the room and then her jailer close the door and lock it. He heard bolts being shot, at the top and bottom of the door.

It was obvious that Manuel would be sitting on a chair outside the door, guarding it in case Anna should try to escape.

Mark lay in wait, listening to Anna move around, getting ready for bed.

In the night air, along with the sound of crickets, he could detect a slow, heartrending sobbing. The poor girl.

He must let her know somehow, but without alerting anyone else, that he had found her.

He walked carefully, silently, and looked around him. There, at his feet was a small tree, covered in white fragrant bell-like flowers. He reached up, plucked a bunch and pulling his hand back, hurled them through the open window.

There was a gasp, a moment's silence, then he saw her very gingerly approach the open window, a light cotton dressing-gown clutched tightly around her.

'Anna, don't say anything,' he whispered. 'Don't make any noise, just come closer to the window. I don't mean you any harm, I've come to save you.'

The sobbing had stopped. She

approached the window and Mark stepped forward to make his presence known.

'Who are you?' She peered at him in the darkness.

'My name's Mark Greenstreet, I'm a policeman. Do you remember me from the hotel in Havana?' he whispered.

'Vaguely.' She held on to the wrought-iron bars at the window. 'You were there the day we checked in, I remember now, at the reception desk. How did you find me? Is Mum OK?'

In a low whisper, he gave her the essentials, then listened as she unfolded to him everything that was going on.

The main thing was she was well, she wasn't harmed. Though it was clear that she was in danger.

'It'll be dawn in a couple of hours,' Mark finally said. 'We'll be back. Don't despair, just stay cool and play your part. Stay strong, you're doing great.'

And with that he was off into the night.

The Stakes are High

When Mark got back to the others, they were still fast asleep. Good. He needed time to think, time to work things through.

Norelvis was like a puppy, Mark noted, lots of fierce and energetic activity but then the ability to collapse and sleep anywhere.

Bryony lay, elegant as a red setter, collapsed from all the stress and strain and the long horse ride.

He looked tenderly on her curled up form, it gave him some relief from the enormity of the task ahead.

It was a while since Mark had looked on a sleeping woman and it was a pleasure he had missed. He realised, as he stood leaning against a tree, gathering his wits about him, that his marriage had been going pear-shaped for some time.

Those quiet moments of contempla-
tion, where you look on someone and
really care for them, had all but gone
from his life.

But he enjoyed looking at Bryony.
Whether scrubbed of make-up like
today, or in a dress, out for an evening
like she had been last night, she was
truly beautiful. Because it didn't matter
what she wore or what time of the day
it was, she was flawless and real, a
natural beauty.

As a moth went near her, he shooed
it away. Without even realising it, it
dawned on him that he had become
smitten.

It might just be, thought Mark wryly,
that finding Bryony's daughter, making
Bryony happy and giving her a reason
to smile again could be the saving of
him.

★ ★ ★

As night deepened, Mark heard the
nocturnal frogs singing their strange

song to the bold moon. As he sat himself down, a spider with furry legs walked on to his trousers.

Just as he was about to brush it off, a small green lizard came stalking from under the leaves, sat for a second or two, sizing up its prey then pounced, chomping up the spider before scooting off.

All life was here, small dramas being played out whilst his brain tried to work out how to deal with their major drama.

The stakes were high for him. He had fallen for Bryony and he was the one who could make or break this mission to bring Anna back safely.

One thing was sure, Mark could not permit Norelvis and Bryony to rest any longer.

'Wake up.' Mark shook first Norelvis, then Bryony. 'I've something to tell you. I've found Anna.'

Mark told them everything. The relief on Bryony's face was as if a cloud had shifted from in front of the sun.

But, as Mark's story unfolded, she

didn't know whether to laugh or cry. For although Anna had been found, they still had to find out how to get her out of there alive.

'One thing I have decided is that we can't get her out without help. Not if they've got an armed guard. Weber obviously means business and will stop at nothing. It's time we involved the police.'

Norelvis shook his head vigorously.

'The Havana police have done nothing so far to find Anna; they drags their feet. I do not trust them.'

'Who can we trust then?'

'Why, the Trinidad police, of course. My schoolfriend's uncle, Davido, is very high in Trinidad police though it is small unit.

'I can telephone, speak to Davido now. Dawn will come soon. He and his two officers have motorbike. They can move quicker than we did on horses. They can park on other side of ridge and walk over. They could be here just before dawn.'

'OK,' Mark said, 'please phone them now.'

After a swift phone conversation in Spanish, Norelvis nodded.

'They pleased to come. Trinidad is sleepy place, they have little excitement except lost cows and stolen boats on the beach. They coming straightaway, with guns.'

* * *

While they waited, Mark tried to figure what was going on and slot together the missing pieces.

'We have to save not just Anna, but also the old lady. I'm sure she's as much a pawn in this game as your daughter,' he said to Bryony. 'What Weber is up to, though, isn't clear. He's obviously using Anna, but how? Perhaps it's some sort of secret the old lady has which he has to worm out of her.

'It sounded to me like he fears she might be in the first stages of dementia, and that if he doesn't find out soon what he needs to know, then it'll be too late.'

'But how did Anna get mixed up in all this?' Bryony asked.

It was on the tip of Mark's tongue to tell Bryony about Warren's gambling and his selling of art on the side. Mark was sure her deceased husband was involved, but until he knew all the facts, he couldn't bring himself to open up to Bryony. What good would it do, when he didn't know how this all fitted together?

While they talked in the darkness Norelvis had gone down to meet the police so he could guide them up to where Mark and Bryony were hiding.

Bryony looked tortured.

'Was there anything else that you saw that could explain what's going on? Nothing in the house?'

'I didn't get a good look, I was too concerned about staying hidden. There was something, now I can think about it clearly, something odd. I barely got to see into the dining-room at all, but, on the wall above the dining-table was a large portrait of a young girl. She had an uncanny resemblance to Anna.

'Her hair was done differently; I think that's what threw me. The girl in the painting had an old-fashioned pinned-up hairdo and a fancy cocktail dress. So unlike Anna, who's always in her jeans and T-shirts and her hair worn loose. But the face was similar, very similar.'

They were left to ponder on that, until finally, the hint of light in the sky beckoned over the hills.

Suddenly, there was the rustle of footsteps through the undergrowth. It was Norelvis, together with a heavily moustached middle-aged man, short of breath, with two younger men. All wore light denim shirts and grey berets with gunbelts slung round their waists. Fresh and energetic, the policemen looked as though they were relishing some action.

Norelvis, too, was wired and ready.

'I explain to Davido what occurred. He says we to follow him and these polices.' Norelvis nodded towards the two officers., 'Santiago and Luis. But we hide at back of house, wait for them to bring out the German Mr Otto, and save Miss Anna.'

For a moment, Mark frowned while he gathered his thoughts.

He wasn't happy leaving it entirely up to the Cubans. They might well be good policemen, but there were only three of them.

Then he pursed his lips with determination. He had his own plan for what to do while they stormed the front of the house.

As the police approached the house, Mark, Norelvis and Bryony were motioned to wait in the bushes while Davido and his men crept around the front. All was silent in the half light, apart from a cockerel crowing way across the valley.

Mark knew that surprise was the best form of defence in such situations. He didn't like the thought of the back of the house being undefended.

'Keep an eye out for me,' he whispered very quietly to the others. 'I'm going up that tree; there's an open window on the first floor I can get through.

'At least, that way, I'll be near Anna's bedroom when the police go in. She'll be terrified, not knowing what's going on. I can help her out from there if needs be.'

'Mark.' Bryony's face was taut with worry.

It was as if she wanted to say something but couldn't. The situation was too tense, the stakes too high.

'Oh, just be careful. Really careful, please. I couldn't bear it if . . . ' Her eyes were full, her knuckles white.

If what? If he should come to some harm, if he should disappear from her life the way Warren had, suddenly, shockingly?

Was it possible she cared for Mark the way he had come to care for her?

He held out his hand, and she gripped it tightly, and in that moment it

207

was as if he was being supplied with liquid energy, straight from her veins into his.

The Truth is Out

Bryony watched on tenterhooks as Mark scaled the tree. Strong arms, strong legs; a large man but surprisingly nimble. Her heart sank. What if he slipped, what if someone inside heard him and . . . ?

It didn't bear thinking about. And Anna? Would he be able to get her out before Otto Weber's guard realised the house was surrounded?

Without warning, there was a loud crack, and Bryony nearly jumped three foot in the air. Gunshots, from the front of the house! Her eyes darted to where Mark had been. He'd disappeared.

Norelvis went to run forward, but Bryony held him back. She couldn't cope if something went wrong and the youngster came to harm. How could she face his mother, knowing that

Norelvis was only here in their bid to save Anna?

Bryony was in a state, not knowing what to do for the best. Were they needed inside, or would they simply be putting themselves in danger?

As if pulling a rabbit from a hat, Mark appeared at the top floor window with Anna and waved to Bryony. The guard must have gone to check on the gunshots, while Mark broke into her room.

He ushered Anna out and she crawled across the branches of the banyan tree and on to the ground where she dashed towards her waiting mother.

Mark followed closely, running to save his life, gunshots ringing from inside the house. Bryony ran to her daughter and folded Anna into her arms, pulling her back into the safety of the undergrowth.

Still shots rang out, crows awakened from their perches in the trees and flapped about the air squawking in the mayhem. Anna sobbed uncontrollably. The terrific din had started every dog in the valley barking at the top of their voices.

Then men were shouting, until suddenly they stopped. Bryony and Anna stood open-mouthed, waiting for what was to come next.

Had Otto Weber and his guard somehow managed to triumph? Had they overpowered the police, or had the police got their man?

Mark started to run to the side of the house, but he didn't need to. There, plain as day, being walked around to meet them, was Otto Weber, fat and waddling, his sausage-like fingers held high in the air.

He was vanquished, with Davido triumphantly walking behind him, his gun pressed into Weber's back.

Next to Davido walked Luis. He pushed the guard, now disarmed, in front of them.

The other officer, Santiago, his face wreathed with smiles, followed with his gun trained on the two criminals. All the policemen nodded to each other; they'd done their job well.

'Look, Mr Mark!' Norelvis yelled. 'All is well. We got them.'

All Bryony knew was that Anna was safe and well. She had no cuts or bruises, though she was shaking in her mother's arms. They held each other so tight, like they would never let go.

When Mark came over, Bryony's eyes filled with tears of relief.

'Oh, thank you, Mark. Thank you so much. How can we ever repay you?'

He nodded, then put his hands on his knees, bending down to relax the tenseness in his neck and shoulders, stretching.

When he straightened up, he finally gave her one of those elusive smiles, and at long last, all seemed well with her world.

Nothing could go wrong now, could it? Not only did she have Anna back, but she had found this wonderful, caring man. She didn't think she'd ever wanted another relationship, no-one else could match up to her near-perfect husband.

But looking at Mark and all he'd risked to help her she might, she decided, have found someone as good as Warren.

Or possibly, even better.

★ ★ ★

The next 24 hours went by in a whirlwind. The police took them back to Havana in a police car and Otto Weber and the old lady, who it was confirmed was his aunt, were taken in a separate squad car.

Norelvis was full of excitement, having taken on the unofficial role of police interpreter. He had been told by Davido what was going to happen next. While they sped along the motorway, he explained.

'We go to Otto Weber's house in Havana for police to search. They not know exactly what his motive in stealing Miss Anna. But the old lady, she know, she says she will show them. We go, too, for you must find out what has been going on and as Davido is uncle of my friend we get special treatment,' he said glowing with pride at his new-found VIP status.

Bryony had not pressed Anna for explanations. The girl clearly needed a rest from her ordeal.

'I haven't slept properly since I last saw you, Mum, I'm exhausted. Please let me sleep on the journey back. There are things I don't understand myself.

'All I can tell you is, Otto Weber kidnapped me because he wanted me to play a part to trick that poor old lady. I had to pretend to be her grandchild, who she hadn't seen for years. I felt awful, but if I didn't he told me he'd reveal the truth about . . . '

'About what, sweetheart? About someone?'

Then Anna's expression had filled with dread. Bryony was confused. What was more, Mark looked so grave. His mouth was pinched and his forehead harsh, with a line of concern which scared her.

'Mark, what's going on?'

'I think it would be best if we wait for Otto Weber to explain what's been going on, and if we let Anna get some rest.'

'Mum, please, Mark's right.'

They exchanged a look, and Anna gripped Bryony's hand very tightly as she laid her head on her shoulder.

'Let me sleep. I'm so tired, so very tired.'

She did sleep the whole journey, while Bryony stared out of the window, not knowing what more shocks the day could hold.

Finally, they reached Havana and the police drove them straight to Otto Weber's house. The door was opened by the maid who looked terrified to see the police.

However, Bryony thought, also in an odd way, she seemed to be expecting them. There was a resigned look on her face as if she might have held herself in readiness for this moment to come at any time.

She gave Otto Weber a look of pure venom, and immediately shot forward to help the old lady over the threshold.

'Come,' Norelvis said. 'We are all to go upstairs, to the room at the top. There is a lift for the old lady but it is too small for all, we must walk.'

Once they had made it to the upstairs room, Bryony gripped Anna's hand tight. Weber's maid, his aunt, Mark, Anna and herself, were all present, then the three policemen marched Weber in, his hands cuffed behind his back.

The old lady took the only seat. She looked exhausted.

'My English is not perfect,' she began with a slight German accent, 'but I have to say how sorry I am that you have been pulled into this dreadful business by my nephew, Otto Weber.

'Here,' she said, fixing him with steely grey eyes and pointing towards the small door leading to the attic, 'is what you were looking for, Otto. Through that door is what you have been hungering for, for decades. The paintings are here. All of them, the whole collection.'

He looked mystified and horrified at the same time. Colour rose in his face, the redness betraying years of pent-up anger.

'They cannot possibly be here,' he spat. 'I've shared this house on and off with you for years, and I have searched in that attic and found nothing. You're lying.'

'No.' She nodded her head. 'Galicia,' she said to the maid, 'go and get the Matisse. That is the finest of the treasures, although, as you know, Otto, there is a Dix, and even a Picasso.'

The maid disappeared into the attic space, then came out with a vibrant painting of a cat chasing a butterfly.

Otto Weber's eyes grew large. He moved his arms as if to touch it, before remembering they were handcuffed. He was bound as surely as a lobster with its claws tied.

'But . . . ' he spluttered. 'I looked everywhere! I searched that attic, the whole house, from top to bottom.'

'You think you're very clever, Otto,' his aunt said. 'But you are not. Just like you thought you were clever kidnapping this girl and persuading her to pretend to be little Marlene, all grown up.

'Yes, it is true I haven't ever seen Marlene, and I haven't even been sent a photo of her grown up. And yes, this girl does look a little like I would imagine my great-niece looks now, she has a certain resemblance to our family. But that's a coincidence.

'The problem is, Otto, I've never trusted you. I never will. I know how duplicitous you are, and how hungry you've always been to find those paintings. I hadn't worked out your plan completely, but I suspected this girl wasn't who she said she was. What's more, I'm not as feeble-minded as I led you to believe. In fact, though, like anyone my age, I do on occasion forget things, my mind is as sharp as ever. It needed to be, with you interfering in my life.'

'What paintings?' Bryony asked, looking at Weber. 'What paintings were so important that you kidnapped my daughter and put us through all this misery?'

It was his aunt who replied.

'It's an important collection, my father's collection. I'm not proud of it, that is why I've never let the paintings see the light of day. They have brought this family nothing but misery and a trail of deception.'

The old lady sighed, and there was the sense that finally she was unburdening herself of a lifetime of secrets.

'My father was an art dealer in Germany in the nineteen-thirties,' she continued. 'A gifted man, he bought and sold legitimately. However, when Hitler came to power, one of the ways he persecuted those he oppressed, and lined the pockets of his henchmen, was to sanction the acquisition of a great deal of art from many Jewish families.

'My father sadly got caught up in this. I'm ashamed to say dear Papa was driven by Goebbels, who had conveniently identified what he described as 'degenerate art'. Many of these beautiful artworks Goebbels thought were 'rubbish', and he and other Nazis could see that here was a way of making money. They persuaded legitimate dealers like my father to acquire such works at knockdown prices.

'These people were desperate to get out of Germany, they needed money to escape. Their collections were devalued and bought for next to nothing, virtually stolen. This was the Nazis' insurance so that they would be rich whatever the outcome of the war.

'My father was in the process of shipping one of these collections at the command of a well-known Nazi general when the general was killed. My father was terrified of what would happen, and feared he would be imprisoned after the war if his part in this hideous practice was ever found out. So he simply hid the paintings here in Cuba.'

She turned to her nephew.

'You knew they existed, Otto, because he told you. But you didn't know where they were hidden. What Papa did to hide his tracks was buy not just this house, but also the house next door. He put a brass plaque on the door, filled it with boring books about trains and pretended to turn it into the headquarters of the Society for the Preservation of Steam Locomotives of Cuba. No such society exists. It was a front, a place for him to hide the paintings.

'Now I suppose, dear Otto, you would like to know exactly where. The paintings are, in fact, located in the attic of that building, not this one. However, there is a secret trapdoor under the floor from the attic of this house, into the attic of the house next door. My father was a clever man, much more so than you will ever be, Otto.'

Otto was fuming, his face shiny with sweat, his nostrils flared.

'Those paintings,' he said through gritted teeth. 'What good were they to you? You were never going to sell them. You could have made me rich.'

'What, and enabled you to be more of a crook than you already are? No, Otto. For years you pretended to care for me, when all you really care for is yourself. But when I got a little forgetful on occasions, you convinced yourself your poor old aunt was getting dementia, and that scared you, didn't it? Because you thought I might go crazy and my secret would die with me.

'That's when you upped your efforts and blackmailed this poor young woman into pretending she was my long-lost granddaughter. My estranged daughter's child, come all the way from Germany to find me.

'I am sorry, child, that you were dragged into this sorry situation. It must have been terrifying. But I am old, I could not fight my corner. I was in fear for myself. I could only sit back and wait and hope the police did their job. Thank goodness they have, finally.'

Otto Weber spoke up.

'The trouble with you, Aunt, is you never really cared for me. You took me on when Mama fell ill all those years ago, only because you had to. It was my sister Clara who was the golden child, the beautiful one. I was ungainly, with none of her artistic talents. She was the one, too, who you wanted to mould into an image of yourself because you had musical aspirations to be a great pianist. But your talent and your application wasn't good enough.

'You took the easy life out when you married Borden. Your rich husband kept you in a lovely lifestyle — big houses, fine holidays. But then, when you couldn't have children and your sister was ill, you leaped on the chance to use Clara as your means of fulfilling your ambition to get involved in the life of a concert pianist. You tried to mould her into the person you had failed to become.'

He shook his head.

'Poor Clara . . . I used to envy and pity her at the same time. Getting all your attention was a double-edged sword. Hours of lessons when she was a child, all that practising and smothering kisses. While I remained in the background, with not a musical note in my head, being ignored. Do you not wonder at my feeling sour towards you?

'What a disappointment for you when Clara decided to go and live in Germany with that husband of hers you never liked. When she had a child of her own and gave up her professional career you decided to disown her. Suddenly she was of no more interest. All that so-called love you had poured into her turned into a need for revenge on her for raising your hopes then dashing them.'

He leaned forward.

'That's why you were so eager to meet her daughter after all these years, wasn't it? That's why, when I told you that little Marlene was turning into a young woman and finally wanted to bury the hatchet and to meet you, you leaped at the chance. Do you know, Aunt, the only bit of good luck I had in my life was to be shown photographs of this young woman, Anna, by her father.'

At this point, Bryony's jaw dropped. Warren? How on earth could he be mixed up in all this?

She turned to Anna, looking for an explanation, but the girl merely dropped her gaze to the floor. It was then that Bryony realised Anna had known something dreadful about her father which she hadn't been able to confess.

Alone With Her Memories

As Bryony listened to Otto Weber continue, she had the sensation that she was falling apart gradually, slowly. That her life would never be the same again.

'Warren Kemp and I did some business together, buying and selling a few paintings. We got to know each other well. When he sent me a photo of Anna I was struck by how much she looked like Clara when she was young.

'That's when I got my idea. Warren was desperate: he'd got himself into financial scrapes, his gambling had got out of hand.'

'Gambling?' Bryony said, aghast.

'You didn't know?' Weber shrugged his shoulders. 'That's not unusual. Often the wife is the last one to know. He needed money and I promised him Anna wouldn't come to any harm.

'He was going to persuade her to play

the part, that's why he arranged for you all to come on holiday here. Then, he said, you were not interested in art, but he could take Anna off ostensibly on little trips to galleries. That is when we would persuade her to pretend to be the long-lost child. She spoke German like a native; it was perfect.'

His eyes widened.

'When Warren died I thought our plan would come to nothing. But then I ran into you that day you arrived in Havana. I couldn't believe my luck that you had still decided to holiday here. I couldn't pass up the opportunity to carry out my plan.

'It was even more perfect because Anna didn't want to besmirch her father's memory in your eyes, dear lady. She didn't want her mother to know that her father was not quite the upright man he pretended to be. It wasn't difficult to persuade her.

'You, Aunt, despite your brave words, weren't entirely sure whether Anna was genuine or not. I think you were biding your time. If she had been genuine, you thought you could still triumph. That you could pay Clara back for deserting you, for the fact you wasted all that time and effort and smothering love you put into her when she was a child.

'I don't believe you weren't taken in. I believe you had your doubts, but you simply weren't sure.'

The old lady shaded her eyes.

'You were very struck at the thought of getting revenge, of being able to steal the girl you thought was Marlene, weren't you? I believe you were taken in, and were on the verge of trying to bring her under your wing. You're lonely, Aunt; you were on the brink of trying to tempt her with money from the paintings, maybe even persuading her to move to Cuba and live with you, now the country is letting foreigners in. You had dreams of installing her in Havana, or even in your mausoleum of a house in Trinidad, and turning her against her mother like you turned against poor Clara all those years ago.

'I thought I could persuade Anna to join in my deception by promising her a cut of the wealth. Once we had got to know where the paintings were, she could have had her money and gone back to England. But the stupid girl wasn't interested, were you, Anna?'

He cast a glance towards Bryony, and she held Anna closer to her than ever.

Mark stepped forward to stand between them. Even in handcuffs, Otto Weber was trying to menace others, to exercise his power to manipulate.

'That was when I had to threaten her,' Otto sneered. 'I had to tell her that I would reveal to her mother what a waster her father was. How he had spent most of his time gambling and living on the edge, and how he had sold stolen goods to feed his habit.'

Bryony suddenly felt sick. What was he saying? What had Warren got himself mixed up in? But Otto Weber carried on.

'Anna didn't believe me at first, did you?'

Bryony turned towards her daughter, but Anna appeared crestfallen, desperately sad at the revelations she could see were searing into Bryony's fond memories of her husband.

'Is he telling the truth, Anna?'

'Mum, I'm so sorry. Dad asked me not to tell. He said it would all be all right in the end, he just had a few debts to pay, then he'd stop.'

'Of course it's true,' Weber scoffed. 'It would have gone according to plan, if this hero in shining armour hadn't turned up.'

He stared at Mark, and if looks could kill Mark would have dropped dead on the spot.

'If you hadn't found me in Trinidad and blown my cover all of this could have ended simply. I would have got what I wanted and this dear lady here would not have had to learn an uncomfortable truth about her dead husband.

'Aunt, I think you would have told us where the paintings were eventually.

Now, none of us can make use of them. Your selfish ways have meant that they will have to go back to Germany, to the families who thought they were gone for ever.'

Mark stepped forward.

'Isn't that what should happen? Those paintings were stolen from their rightful owners. They may have been bought, but they were bought in wartime at ridiculously low prices from people who were desperate. They were, in effect, stolen and they've never done either of you any good. You two are as bad as each other. I think we've heard enough here today.'

With that, Davido, the Trinidad police chief, led Otto Weber away, leaving his two officers Luis and Santiago to clear the paintings out of the house and take them under armed guard to the police station.

As they departed from the building, leaving Otto Weber's aunt alone in her big house with just her faithful maid to look after her, Bryony looked back and for a moment felt a pang of compassion for the sad old lady.

She'd been left alone with her memories. Now she had no family, not even Otto for company. She was left with nothing but the misery that selfishness and deviousness brings. Nevertheless, the last Bryony saw of her, was her looking out of the window with her chin defiantly raised.

Pain and Anger

Bryony had her own demons to deal with. She felt wrung out and exhausted, mentally and physically.

As they were taken back to the hotel in the police car, they all sat in silence. When they got out, there was an awkward pause as they stood on the pavement waiting to go in. Bryony couldn't hold back any longer, as another awful truth had dawned on her.

'You knew, didn't you, Mark?' she demanded. 'You knew Warren had somehow been mixed up in this and you didn't tell me. Why didn't you tell me?'

'There were good reasons.'

'There can never be good reasons for keeping silent about something like that. Warren's dead, for goodness sake.'

The word fell hard on the sultry Havana air. There, she'd said it. She'd named it for what it was.

Before, she'd used the euphemisms we all use: passed away, deceased, widowed. It was as if not saying it could stop it from hurting her. Now, everything was unwrapped and raw.

'To find out, when I was coming to terms with Warren's death, that he lied to me, that he was living a double life and . . . ' Bryony gulped ' . . . and that you, who I trusted, lied to me is the worst thing of all. Especially when I was just beginning to trust a man again.'

She realised it was inappropriate to be pouring out her heart on the street like this, where tourists turned to stare and even the doorman was looking embarrassed.

But she didn't care. She'd spent years being good, being the dutiful, quiet wife.

Perhaps it was something about Cuba and its tropical down-to-earth attitude, where life was lived out on the streets. So what if she said what she thought out loud? So what if she was shouting, gesticulating, if her hair was wild and her fists clenched?

'You treated me like a child, Mark. Did you think I couldn't take it? Believe me, I've taken a lot over the last few years, and I've survived and I will continue to survive — despite people lying to me!'

'Mum.' Anna put out a hand to console her.

'No, don't try to calm me down!' Bryony snapped, waving her away. 'I've never been so angry and I need to get this out.'

With that, Bryony turned on her heel, sped into the hotel, rushed up to her room and hurled herself on the bed.

She didn't care that she'd made a scene. She didn't care that she'd been selfish and loud and unreasonable. Just for once she would darn well let it all out. Say what she thought, stand up for herself; be her own person rather than Anna's mother or Warren's wife or Mark's . . .

Mark's what?

She sat up. What was Mark to her? Or rather, what had he been? For she was sure he would never want to see her again. He'd never want to talk to her even or help her after the way she'd exploded like that.

A friend? A potential boyfriend? That was why she'd just behaved so badly. When Warren had gone from her life she had sworn she couldn't cope with such pain again. Sworn never to have feelings for another man.

Mark had opened a chink in her armour. Made her think that perhaps she might feel again, that she might even love again. What had she lost by baring her soul, by being unguarded and saying exactly what came into her head?

Bryony went into the bathroom and deluged her face with cold water. Then she rested her hands on the basin and stared at herself in the mirror. Her world was imploding. She didn't know who or what to believe any more.

How could she ever trust again? She

couldn't. She was so done with men lying to her. She had never felt so totally and utterly miserable and alone.

There was a knock on the door. Bryony's heart leaped. Had Mark forgiven her for her outburst? Could he be coming up to make sure she was all right, to protect and heal her, to say she'd got it all wrong somehow?

Instead, it was Anna. She had two large cocktails, one in each hand. One in layers of red, yellow and orange, the other in layers of green, blue and turquoise. Both had jaunty umbrellas propped in them and slices of pineapple. Happy, jolly, holiday drinks. Seeing them, and her daughter, just made Bryony want to cry again.

'Come on, Mum, get one of these down you and I guarantee the world won't seem like such a difficult place.'

All the times Bryony had urged her daughter not to drown her sorrows in alcohol! But for once, Bryony did just that. She grabbed them both and took a long swig, first from the one that looked like a sunset, and then another huge swig from the one which looked like the Caribbean sea.

'Steady, Mum!' Anna managed a laugh. 'Leave some for me. You are in a bad way, aren't you?

'Mum, please don't be sad, and don't be too hard on Mark. We both sort of lied to you, I guess.'

Mother and daughter sat on the bed together. In the early evening light, a salsa bar on the roof of the hotel opposite had started to drum out its intoxicating rhythms.

The chilled cocktails slowly made their way to Bryony's fingertips and in no time at all had reached her toes. She lay back, breathing more steadily now, with the warmth of Anna laid next to her. They chomped their way through the pineapple slices, and each had one of the cherries on sticks. The sugary fruits were comforting, like nursery food.

'Why did you lie, Anna? Why couldn't you have told me about Dad and what he was up to?'

'How could I? He was in trouble, and he swore me not to tell. Said it would all be all right. Just that he'd got this bit of a habit with the gambling and it had got out of hand but he could handle it, he had a plan, he could sort it but only if I helped.

'It was all legitimate, he said. Those paintings he reckoned had been promised to Otto Weber by his uncle, they'd been written up in a will. It was just that Otto Weber's aunt didn't like him and had destroyed her husband's will. He said we weren't going to hurt anyone or anything and that just one of the paintings would be enough to solve Otto's and Dad's problems. If I told you, you would be devastated and it would cause ructions.'

Tears filled her eyes.

'I'm so sorry, Mum, I didn't know which way to turn, what with that and my exams and everything. That's one of the reasons I just found I couldn't eat any more. I felt sick half the time just thinking about it. I'm so sorry I worried you.'

Bryony pulled her close to, and kissed the top of her head, sniffing in the wonderful, familiar scent of her own child.

It was a scent she was eternally grateful for and of which she would never tire.

'It wasn't your fault, lovey, none of it was down to you. You were just being a dutiful daughter. I know your dad was very persuasive, in lots of ways. He had that way about him. If he wanted something he'd go all out to get it and he wouldn't give up, he just wore you down.

'I'm just sorry he lost his way, and I'm sorry he was too wrapped up in his own other life to confide in me. I suppose he knew I'd put a stop to it straight away. It was wrong of him to involve you. He knew you couldn't say no, that you loved him too much.'

Anna nodded.

'Then, after he died,' she said, 'it

would have seemed cruel to tell you the truth, Mum. What would have been the point? And I never thought for one moment that we would run into Otto Weber in Cuba, but then I didn't realise that the centre of Havana's such a small space. It's not like London, is it?'

'No, darling, not at all.'

'Do you want another drink, Mum?'

'Why not?'

They ordered a second cocktail from room service, after which Bryony watched Anna fall slowly off to sleep. The evening sky turned from azure to navy blue, then became sprinkled with stars.

Bryony's head was thumping, her skull felt tight after so many tears. She needed some fresh air.

She wrote a brief note to Anna.

Gone for a little walk down the Malecón to clear my head. I've got my mobile. Be back soon.

She slipped it under Anna's hand and quietly let herself out of the room.

A Love Worth Waiting For

The air blowing off the sea was exactly what Bryony needed. When you've found a new love and then lost it, there's very little that can make life seem bearable, but a warm night on Havana's seafront provided a little balm to her aching heart.

She would never know if Mark might have been the one to make her whole again. She'd blown it. She was alone once again.

Anna would soon go off to live her own life, have her own boyfriend, get married one day, have children.

Bryony strolled disconsolately in the sparkling night. Lovers sat on the Malecón wall, hand in hand, their heads nuzzled together. Bright lights blinked across the water, shining in the dark night.

One girl and her boyfriend cuddled

their poodle between them, the picture of togetherness. Another girl lay with her head in her boyfriend's lap as he ran her long raven black hair through his hands like water.

A guy in white jeans and sleeveless white T-shirt, skin caramel coloured like demerara, his biceps strong and prominent, played a trumpet while a group of *salseros* danced the night away.

Street sellers hawked sweet fried bananas and homemade lemonade from rickety wheeled carts. Hopeful fishermen dipped their rods into the waves.

People were surrounded by friends, relatives, acquaintances, lovers. In this vibrant crazy city no-one seemed to be alone — apart from Bryony.

She wandered aimlessly until she felt she could wander no more. Turning round, she retraced her steps in a daze, wondering where and when her life had got so complicated and all gone so very wrong.

In the crowd of people, she suddenly

saw a familiar outline. A tall, white-shirted, broad-shouldered figure, his face serious, his gait determined. Mark.

She looked around for somewhere to escape, somewhere to hide. She didn't need that complication in her life.

He would confront her, tell her how unreasonable she was, tell her that as a policeman he knew when to keep quiet and when people should be told things.

Assured, confident and practical, he didn't need raging angry women in his life. What's more, how could she have betrayed all his help by yelling at him like a banshee?

She turned on her heels and quickened her pace. A sea of people advanced towards her as the night-time crowds on the *Malecón* reached their zenith. Bryony longed to be swallowed up, to disappear in this collection of people, to get lost and be on her own.

Salsa music bombarded her and a wave suddenly crashed in from the unquiet sea and sprinkled her with salt water. There was a gap in the wall, down on to the rocks which bordered the shore. Small groups were gathered on them, mingling happily with their friends and family, chatting and having fun.

With difficulty, Bryony scrambled over the rocks towards the water. The ocean beckoned, it was closer here, the waves swelling in the blackness.

Someone called to her in Spanish. Were they warning her that it was too rough, that she shouldn't go any nearer the ocean? She didn't care, she just wanted the quiet, the darkness, the solitude.

Surely it was better, safer, to be alone, not to be connected to any man?

Men were too complicated. They lied, they pretended to be what they were not, and they died. Without warning. They left you to fend for yourself. Sometimes, even after death they failed you, betrayed you, brought you trouble and pain, haunted your dreams.

Suddenly, Bryony felt her shoulders

being grabbed and she was spun round. There before her stood Mark.

Her heart pounded as if the salsa rhythm had invaded her bloodstream. He was glowing with sweat, the taut sinews of his neck and his fine bone structure glowed in the light from the shore. His chest rose and fell from running, from scrambling over the rocks to stop her going further.

'Where on earth do you think you're going?'

'I don't know; I don't know.' She shook her head.

His hands were hot and firm on her shoulders. Her feet were damp from the sea spray, her white cotton skirt clinging to her legs.

'Bryony, please, don't run like this.'

'Why shouldn't I? How can I carry on after all that's happened? How could you do that, Mark, how could you have stayed silent, how could you keep all that stuff from me? I'm not a child.'

'No, no, you're clearly not that. You're a woman, a beautiful, lively, brave, wonderful woman. Truly you are.'

Bryony shook her head at the words. It was rubbish. She was weak. He was just saying stuff, anything to make her feel good and yet his words had as much value as a torn-up love letter chucked on the raging sea. And like a letter full of empty sentiments and wild protestations, his words were being eaten up by the sound of the waves, swallowed and sent tumbling to the bottom of the ocean for all they meant.

It was over. They were over.

'I'm not a child and you could, you should, have told me what you knew. You kept things from me, you lied. How could I ever trust you? With Warren lying to me and now you, I can't trust any man.'

'Oh, Bryony.' Mark held his head, then he raised it and his clear, honest eyes shone with need.

Another wave crashed on the rocks and drenched them. They didn't move, they were too wrapped up in each another.

'I'm so, so sorry,' he said. 'I would have told you; I was waiting for the right time, when everything was over, when it was all resolved and Anna was back again.

'Please,' he urged as she turned her face away, salt spray dripping from her hair.

Tenderly, he took a hand to brush it away from her eyes.

'Please believe me. I wasn't treating you like a child. I had only half the information, I wanted to check it out properly. I knew you'd be devastated, knew you'd have questions.

'What's more, I've seen plenty of people going through situations like yours, dealing with loved ones who have disappeared and I know that even the strongest people only have so much strength. Then one small thing tips them over, just because it's all too much.

'You needed to be strong in order to

find Anna. You needed to have all your reserves ready so you could trek through the jungle on a horse, so you could spend a night in the jungle. I needed to keep you strong.

'What Warren did was history, it couldn't be changed. You may think I did wrong and I apologise from the depth of my being for that. But I stand by my reasons that you had too much on your plate and I didn't have all the facts and for that reason it was right to wait.

'I've actually finally had a report faxed to me from the police in England, it's at the hotel now. It tells the whole sorry story of what Warren was up to. Now is the right time for you to know, not yesterday, or the day before or the day I heard it. Now, when Anna's safe, when Otto Weber is securely behind bars.'

His tone softened.

'Now, when I can tell you the truth — that I've fallen in love with you, Bryony. Whether you love me or loathe me I have to tell you, because there's a right time for everything and now is the right time for me to say those words because I simply can't hold back. I love you.'

★   ★   ★

Bryony peered at him in the half light, his hand warm on her cheek, the ocean ebbing and flowing, the street with all its crush of people and colours and throbbing noise.

But she was aware of nothing other than the man in front of her, standing firm, like an oak tree, strong, nurturing, passionate, unbending in his need to do what was right and what he was compelled to do.

Mark, with his serious, deep eyes; with his firm lovely body, Mark, with his principles running through him like the granite running through the rocks they stood on.

In an uncertain world which swirled and rolled like the ocean around her, there was Mark, standing up for what he believed in whilst showing her the inner core of softness, warmth, hot blood, male need and longing.

For her. All for her.

Finally, her breath short, her pulses ticking, and her heart melting, Bryony managed to find a tiny smile.

Perhaps everything wasn't lost, after all. Five minutes ago, totally alone, she'd wondered if she'd ever smile again.

'Mark, I . . . I'm sorry too. I'm sorry I was so quick to condemn you. I was hurting so, so much.'

'You don't have to hurt any more.' He cupped her face in his hands. He bent down so she could feel the warmth of his skin on her cheek.

He brought his lips to hers and in an instant she could hear nothing else but his urgent, needful breath of life, she could feel nothing but the pressure of his hands on her shoulders, the salty sweetness of his lips, and instead of hard stone underfoot she felt as if she had been raised up and was floating on the night air.

Her stomach flipped like a dolphin in the sea and she wrapped him in her arms, heard his soft, insistent moan and was lost, totally, and utterly, deliriously and deliciously.

He pulled away.

'Forgive me?' It was part question and part statement.

'If you forgive me for ranting at you.'

'I'm a different man, Bryony, I'm not Warren . . . '

She put her hand to his lips.

'I know. I know that now. That's history. That's forgotten. This is us.'

He smiled, then bent down, swept her up in his arms and carried her over the rocks towards the land, towards the light.

Towards the music, towards life, towards love; towards the future.

We do hope that you have enjoyed reading this large print book.

Did you know that all of our titles are available for purchase?

We publish a wide range of high quality large print books including:
Romances, Mysteries, Classics
General Fiction
Non Fiction and Westerns

Special interest titles available in large print are:
The Little Oxford Dictionary
Music Book, Song Book
Hymn Book, Service Book

Also available from us courtesy of Oxford University Press:
Young Readers' Dictionary
(large print edition)
Young Readers' Thesaurus
(large print edition)

For further information or a free brochure, please contact us at:
Ulverscroft Large Print Books Ltd.,
The Green, Bradgate Road, Anstey,
Leicester, LE7 7FU, England.
Tel: (00 44) **0116 236 4325**
Fax: (00 44) **0116 234 0205**

Other titles in the
Linford Romance Library:

DESIGN FOR LOVE

Ginny Swart

With her promotion to assistant art director at Market Media, a lovely new flat, and her handsome steady boyfriend Grant, Andrea Ross's future looks rosy. But when her gentle, fatherly boss decides to retire, and the company hires Luke Sullivan as the new art director, nothing is certain anymore. With a reputation as both a slave driver and a serial charmer of women, he quickly stamps his imprint on the department. Meanwhile, things with Grant aren't exactly going to plan . . .

THE SIGNET RING

Anne Holman

Resigned to spinsterhood, Amy Gibbon is astounded to receive a proposal of marriage from Viscount Charles Chard upon their very first meeting! Love quickly flares in her heart, but Charles is more reticent — he needs an heir, and this is a marriage of convenience. Determined to win her new husband over, Amy follows him to France amid the dangers of the Napoleonic wars, where he must search for his father's precious stolen signet ring. Can true love blossom under such circumstances?

THE LOST YEARS

Irena Nieslony

Upon returning from their honeymoon in Tanzania, Eve Masters and her new husband David are quickly embroiled in chaos. When a hit-and-run accident almost kills them both, David develops amnesia and has no recollection of who Eve is. And then she pays a visit to his first wife — to find her dead body slumped over the kitchen table, with herself as the prime murder suspect! Will Eve be able to solve this tangled web, and will David remember her again — or will the villains win for the first time?

SAFE HAVEN

Eileen Knowles

Taking shelter from a snowstorm, Giselle Warren revisits an isolated holiday cottage, expecting it to be vacant — and walks straight into someone's home instead! Blake Conrad, the owner, has moved in after splitting with his girlfriend. In rocky circumstances of her own with her fiancé, who she suspects wants to marry her purely for her money, Giselle has been hoping for solitude in which to gather her thoughts. But this chance meeting with Blake will change both of their lives forever — after she makes him an incredible proposition . . .

A TOUCH OF THE EXOTIC

Dawn Knox

From India to war-torn London to an estate in Essex, Samira's life is one of rootlessness and unpredictability. With her half-Indian heritage, wherever she goes she's seen as 'exotic', never quite fitting in despite her best efforts. To add to her troubles, her beauty attracts attention from men that she's not sure how to handle. But when she falls for handsome RAF pilot Luke, none of her charms seem to work, as it appears his heart is already bestowed elsewhere . . .